JACK BE QUICK

AND OTHER CRIME STORIES

D0005412

JACK BE QUICK

AND OTHER CRIME STORIES

Barbara Paul

Five Star
Unity, Maine

Acknowledgments may be found on page 219.

Five Star Mystery
Published in conjunction with Tekno Books and Ed Gorman.

Cover photograph by Jason Johnson.

June 1999
Standard Print Hardcover Edition.

Five Star Standard Print Mystery Series.

The text of this edition is unabridged.

Set in 11 pt. Plantin by Minnie B. Raven.

Printed in the United States on permanent paper.

Library of Congress Cataloging in Publication Data

Paul, Barbara, 1931–
    Jack be quick and other crime stories / by Barbara Paul.
        p. cm.
    Okay, Diogenes, you can stop looking — we found him —
Scat — French asparagus — The favor — Portrait of the artist
as a young corpse — Stet — Ho Ho Ho — Play nice —
Jack be quick.
    ISBN 0-7862-1919-X (hc : alk. paper)
    1. Detective and mystery stories, American. I. Title.
PS3566.A82615J3 1999
813´.54—dc21   99-22369

INTRODUCTION

It was with fear and trepidation that I first plunged into writing short stories in the mystery genre. Consider. All the elements of any short story must be included: a plot that builds to a logical climax, believable characters, dialogue that sounds like real speech, etc. The story must be *about* something. If the setting is an exotic locale or some period in the past, you have to work in details of that as well. Add to this the elements of mystery: crime, investigation, solution. And clues . . . you need clues. Even a red herring or two would be nice. But that's a lot, and you don't have much space to fit it all in.

So how do you manage all that? Trial and error? Prayer? A low-fat diet? There must be some secret behind it.

Well . . . not exactly. Each story carries its own demands, and they're never quite the same as any other story's. A writing device that works in one story might not work in the next, etc. It's that special uniqueness that makes the short story form so appealing to me; the possibilities for variety are endless. A different kind of discipline is at work in the short form—different from novel-writing, that is. There's not much room for side trips in the short story, and writing in that format forces you to stick to the subject. That makes it possible to work in that long list of elements I mentioned above. The form of the short story itself is the secret, if there has to be a secret.

When Ed Gorman called and asked me to put this collection together, my first thought was that I wouldn't be able to include "Homebodies" and "Making Lemonade"—

two stories I'm satisfied with (not true of everything I write, by the way). But I couldn't expect people to pay money for those stories when I've been offering them as free downloads from my website for several years. They're still available; you can find both of them at http://www.barbarapaul.com/shortmys.html.

So I've tried to include a mixture in this collection—humorous and serious, long and short. I enjoyed writing every story in this book. I hope you enjoy reading them.

—Barbara Paul

TABLE OF CONTENTS

This story was written for an anthology that had the theme of food and cooking . . . and each contributing writer was asked to provide a recipe related to the story. Well, I'd done the Julia Child thing years ago; but recently I've been spending as little time in the kitchen as possible. So I asked an online buddy, Doug Brewer, for a recipe; he gave me one for Sloshed Chicken (beer marinade). I'd had it in my head to write a story about an honest man whose attempt to do a decent thing involves him in a murder. So I made him an honest man who likes to cook. In fact, it's his purchase of fresh herbs for the Sloshed Chicken that gets him into the mess in the first place.

OKAY, DIOGENES, YOU CAN STOP LOOKING—WE FOUND HIM

All Dennis Ogden wanted was to buy some fresh basil. He needed to start the marinade tomorrow before leaving for work, and there wouldn't be time to go out in the morning. A jar of dried basil stood in Dennis's spice rack . . . but the dried kind just wasn't pungent enough for the dish. He'd run down to Cabot's Food Market and be home again in twenty minutes.

Gloves and muffler; January weather in November. He could have stopped at the Big Bird Supermarket on the way home, but Dennis didn't like supermarkets. Or frozen dinners. Or Chinese take-out. He hadn't had a hot dog in ten years, and pizza was a four-letter word. Dennis Ogden liked his own cooking.

Patches of ice on the sidewalk slowed him down. The windows of Cabot's Food Market were free of steam but inside was toasty-warm. Dennis waved to Louie at the check-out counter and made his way to the produce section. Cabot's was small and their prices were high—but you got what you paid for there. You never had to throw away the outer leaves of a head of lettuce to get to the good part. A pound of their ground beef didn't cook down to a meatball. And their fruits . . . ah, their fruits! The supermarkets all sprayed their fruits with chemicals to make them nice and shiny and to hide the fact that they were utterly tasteless. Cabot's never resorted to such tricks; they didn't have to. Dennis liked Cabot's.

Dennis picked up a couple of plums in addition to the fresh basil. Louie was bagging the groceries of a large man in an unbuttoned black overcoat, who was tugging on a pair of gloves that seemed too small for his big hands. Dennis put his three items down on the check-out counter.

"Hey, Mr. Ogden," Louie said, eyeing the basil. "Greek salad?"

"Not this time. Sloshed Chicken."

The large man in the black coat turned to look at him. " 'Sloshed' Chicken?"

"Beer marinade," Dennis explained.

"I tried that with dill weed once," Louie said, ringing up Dennis's bill. "Couldn't even taste it."

Dennis shook his head. "Dill's too delicate. The other flavors drown it out."

The large man laughed. " 'Sloshed' Chicken." He picked up his bag of groceries.

The two men walked out together. "I'm just learning

about cooking," the large stranger said amiably. "I'm in the midst of a divorce and already sick of eating in restaurants all the time."

"I know what you mean," Dennis replied. "I prefer my own cooking anyway." He patted his middle. "Unfortunately."

"Hmm. I've been frying everything because it's quickest, but I'm going to have to cut that out." The man tried to button his overcoat one-handed but soon gave it up rather than remove his glove.

"Cooking's a good way to wind down at the end of the day," Dennis remarked. "At least for me. I need to wind down after work. Don't you? I do."

The big man backed off. "Well . . . been nice talking to—" His feet flew out from under him and he went down *thunk* flat on his back, right on the patch of ice he'd slipped on.

It took Dennis a moment to react—but then he quickly bent over the fallen man. "Are you hurt? I mean, of course you're hurt . . . that was a nasty fall. But are you hurt badly? Er, seriously?"

The man waved him off weakly. "Winded . . . just give me a . . . minute . . . I'm okay. . . ." He lay with his unbuttoned coat bunched up under the small of his back; it had probably protected him when he hit.

Dennis looked at the groceries scattered all over the sidewalk. He picked up the stranger's blue plastic bag and was gathering up cheese and celery and veal chops when Louie came rushing out of the store. "Omigod! Is he hurt?"

"Just winded." Dennis picked up the last of the stranger's groceries, a loaf of rye bread.

Louie was kneeling by the prone man. "Don't try to get up! Don't move! I'll go call an ambulance!"

The large man struggled to a sitting position. "I'm not

hurt. I just need to catch my breath."

"But you might be injured without knowing it!" Louie went on. "And it could come back to haunt you later! It's better to make sure now . . . I can take you to the emergency room of the hospital, they can check you out—"

Scared of being sued, Dennis thought. "He says he's not hurt, Louie. For heaven's sake, stop fussing!"

Wincing, the man got to his feet. He told Louie not to worry, accepted his groceries from Dennis with thanks, and walked stiffly away . . . watching carefully where he put his feet.

Louie's teeth were chattering from the cold. "I hope he's all right."

"He refused medical treatment. I'm your witness, if that's what you're worrying about. Now, get back inside before you freeze to death."

Louie nodded and hurried back into the store. About half a block away, the big man got into a car and started the engine.

Dennis picked up his own blue plastic bag from where he'd left it . . . and saw something on the sidewalk he'd missed. At first he thought it was a packaged food of some sort, but then he saw it was a billfold. A very fat billfold. Heedless of the ice, he whirled and yelled "Wait!"

But the stranger's car pulled away from the curb and drove off.

Slowly Dennis bent over and picked up the billfold; it was so full it wouldn't close properly. He opened it and gazed wonderingly at the wad of greenbacks it contained. He poked at the money with a gloved finger . . . and saw the bills were of the thousand-dollar denomination.

Without thinking he slapped the billfold against his chest, covering it with his hand. Quickly he glanced through the window of Cabot's Food Market; Louie was already busy with another customer. Dennis looked up and down the street. The only other people in sight were a young couple having an argument down on the corner and most assuredly paying no attention to him. A taxicab drove by . . . rather suspiciously, Dennis thought.

But the cab turned the corner and nobody yelled at Dennis to put that billfold back where he found it. Zombie-like, he headed homeward, his gloved hand still pressing the billfold against his chest. It was only after he'd gone a full block that he thought to put it in a pocket.

At home he shrugged out of his coat and sat down at the kitchen table with the billfold. He took out the thousand-dollar bills, crisp and new and so fresh from the bank they were still sticking together. He counted; fifty of them exactly. Plus four twenties and a one.

Fifty. Thousand. Dollars.

Dennis washed a plum and ate it. Fifty-thousand big ones, fallen out of the sky into his very own lily-whites. Fifty-thousand and eighty-one bucks . . . and nobody saw him pick it up.

A new car. Or a real vacation next summer instead of some economy tour. Or maybe both? Or a new kitchen—oh, yes! Totally refurbished, with a brand new *everything*. Well, maybe not everything; it was only fifty thou, after all.

He tossed the plum pit into the garbage and rinsed the juice off his hands. Then he opened the billfold again and saw the owner of the cash was named Jordan McClure. And Mr. Jordan McClure had credit cards—lots and lots and *lots* of credit cards. If Dennis moved quickly, before the credit cards' owner had time to report them missing—

Dennis sat planning his shopping spree, trying to remember what places stayed open late. Electronics stores.

Televisions, cameras. He could buy as many computers as McClure's credit limit would allow and then resell them later. No clothing . . . that would eat up too much time. Jewelry. Diamonds.

He sighed with pleasure and replaced McClure's money in the billfold. What a lovely, lovely fantasy. Dennis hadn't indulged himself like that in a long time. It would have been fun, buying all those things.

When the glow of his make-believe shopping trip began to fade, Dennis opened the phone book to find Jordan McClure's number. Not listed. He went back to the billfold and checked the man's address . . . about five blocks from Dennis's apartment building. Without giving it another thought, he got back into his winter coat and set out to return McClure's billfold to him with its contents intact.

McClure lived in a house, not an apartment. Dennis hoped the man wouldn't try to give him a reward, or insist on making a public fuss over finding someone honest still left in the world. All of Dennis's acquaintances would consider him a fool for returning the money; he knew that without question. Dennis hated being laughed at.

Odd . . . the front door was ajar. Dennis rang the bell and waited a minute. Feeling strange at doing so, he pushed the door all the way open and stepped inside. "Mr. McClure?" he called. When he got no answer, he called again.

He had a *bad* feeling; people didn't leave their front doors open. They just didn't. Was he going to walk into the next room and find McClure's body sprawled on the floor, a knife sticking out of his chest? Maybe the murderer was still lurking about, waiting to jump him?

Just thinking the thought made him feel absurd; he

squared his shoulders and walked boldly into the living room. Empty.

He checked the dining room, the study, and a small bathroom. Evidently the bedrooms were on the second floor, but Dennis had no intention of going upstairs. He was already uncomfortable, invading the man's privacy like this. He'd just take a peek into the kitchen and then be gone.

And that's where he found Jordan McClure, sprawled out on the floor as envisioned . . . but without the knife sticking out of his chest. Instead, a bullet hole showed clearly at the bridge of his nose. Someone had shot him right between the eyes.

Dennis's knees began to buckle and he sank down on the nearest kitchen chair. He couldn't look at McClure. He found himself focusing on something lying on the kitchen counter: it was the package of veal chops he'd picked up off the sidewalk in front of Cabot's Food Market.

Was the killer still here? Dennis had checked the downstairs, and why would someone kill a man in the kitchen and then go up to the bedrooms? Dennis told himself firmly that the killer had gone.

Gradually his initial shock wore off and he began to think of calling the police. No point in summoning an ambulance; Dennis had never seen anything deader than Jordan McClure. But he'd have to step over McClure's body to reach the kitchen phone . . . euuww. No, he'd find a phone somewhere else in the house.

He didn't want to make the call. He wanted to go home and forget all about Jordan McClure. But he couldn't just walk away and leave the man's body lying there like that. *So get on with it,* he told himself. Dennis rose shakily to his feet . . . and the doorbell rang.

"Jordan?" a woman's voice called out. "Are you home?"

A man's voice added, "Why is the door open?"

Two people were about to walk in and find him with McClure's corpse—and with fifty thousand of McClure's dollars in his pocket.

Dennis did what any normal man would do in such a situation: he panicked. He opened the first door he saw and found himself in a small laundry room. He closed the door behind him and swore when he saw there was no way to lock it from the inside—and no time to go looking for a better hiding place. On the spur of the moment he buried McClure's billfold in a basket of dirty laundry.

Then he prayed.

The newcomers found their way into the kitchen; Dennis listened to their muted voices expressing shock, horror. No one screamed, no one burst into tears. Then followed a long conversation in low tones; Dennis listened hard but couldn't make out what they were saying. But it was clear these two weren't calling the police. He pressed his ear against the door, but all he could hear was the squeaky sound sneakers make on a tile floor.

The door opened so suddenly he almost fell. Dennis gawked wide-eyed at an equally wide-eyed woman, who was oddly dressed in sweats and Reeboks and a fur coat.

"Never mind," the man's voice said. "I found some paper towels."

Dennis and the woman stared at each other a moment, and then her face relaxed into a smile. "Hey, Cappy!" she called out. "Come look at what I found."

"I should have used the dried basil," Dennis said glumly.

They'd moved to the living room.

Cappy turned out to be an overweight, bushy-haired man with a mustache that all but hid his mouth. He was wiping blood from his hand where he'd felt for a pulse. One look was all it took to tell Dennis that this fellow was baaad news. The first thing Cappy had done was to let Dennis see he was carrying a gun. The second thing he'd done was to frisk him.

Dennis had protested. "If you're a cop, show me some I.D.!"

Cappy, the superior bully, had merely snorted. "Don't make me laugh." Satisfied that Dennis was unarmed, he'd taken his billfold and pushed him down on the sofa.

"Who is he?" the woman asked.

Cappy opened the billfold. "Name's Dennis Ogden. Ever heard of 'im?" She shook her head. "Well, Dennis," Cappy said in his grating top-dog manner, "where the hell did you come from and what were you doing hiding in the laundry?"

Dennis sighed. "Hiding in the laundry was stupid. I'd come in right before you did, and . . . and I was afraid I'd be suspected of killing him."

"You're right on that point, Dennis. What did you do with the gun?"

"What gun? I didn't kill him! I don't even own a gun! You're the only one here with a gun!"

"Hey, I didn't off McClure . . . forget that. I got here after you did!"

"You could have killed him earlier and then come back!"

"And you could be lookin' to point the finger at me since *you* got caught in the act!"

"That's enough!" The woman spoke sharply and Cappy fell silent; Dennis couldn't figure out the relationship between these two.

She looked at him a moment and then asked, "What *are* you doing here?"

Dennis had had time to think of a story. "I was coming to dinner."

The woman laughed. "Jordan couldn't cook worth a damn."

"I know," Dennis said in what he hoped was a sincere manner. "But I do cook. I was going to prepare the meal, give him a few tips. We were going to have veal chops." Dennis had stopped eating veal years ago.

"There are veal chops out on the counter," the woman murmured.

"I saw 'em," Cappy snapped. "And he coulda seen 'em too. This guy's no old buddy come for dinner. One of us woulda known him."

"I met Jordan McClure for the first time a few hours ago," Dennis said evenly. "At Cabot's Food Market."

"Oh, and he just comes up to you and says, 'Hey, you look like a good cook—come fix my dinner for me.' "

"Not quite. We got to talking about food." Dennis decided against explaining the Sloshed Chicken. "He said he was in the middle of a divorce and only now learning how to cook. One thing led to another, and I offered to show him a few tricks. That's all there was to it."

Cappy and the woman exchanged a look. She said, "It could have happened like that." The man snorted, said nothing.

Dennis licked his lips. "May I have my billfold back, please."

Cappy tossed it to him but spoke to the woman. "Okay, say this guy is Sir Lancelot. Then who shot your husband?"

"You want me to guess?"

"Yeah, I want you to guess."

"Then I'd guess whoever was blackmailing him."

Blackmail? And this was the grieving widow? "You're Mrs. McClure?" Dennis turned to the man. "Who are you?"

"Arnold Cappy. Private investigator."

"He's working for me," Mrs. McClure said.

Cappy actually handed Dennis a card. "Keep it. You never know when you'll need a private investigator."

The card said *Domestic Cases Our Specialty.* "The way I heard it," Dennis said carefully, "it's the blackmailer who gets murdered, isn't it? Why would a blackmailer shoot his victim? That's killing the goose that lays the golden eggs."

Mrs. McClure threw up her hands. "I don't know! I'm not up on the etiquette of blackmail. I just know that once Jordan had to come up with fifty thousand dollars to pay someone off, and maybe the blackmailer wanted to be paid again."

Fifty thousand dollars. The same fifty thousand that . . . Dennis felt as if someone had just dropped a piano on him. *I killed him! If it weren't for me, he'd still be alive!* If Dennis had returned the money immediately, none of this would have happened. But the blackmailer had showed up to collect, McClure discovered he no longer had the money, the blackmailer got mad and pulled out a gun and shot him! *I could have prevented this! But no, I had to have my little fantasy, I had to hold the money in my hands for a while, I had to play my make-believe little games . . .*

"Why are you sitting there making faces?" Mrs. McClure asked curiously.

Dennis muttered something about indigestion and said, "What line of work was your husband in, Mrs. McClure?"

"Jordan and his partner owned a chain of convenience stores."

Cappy made his hand into a gun and aimed it at her. "That partner. There's your blackmailer. Larry Proctor."

Mrs. McClure waved a hand dismissively. "Larry? He's a pussycat."

"Yeah, well, who else knows enough about your husband to blackmail him? You and Proctor, you're the only ones.

And I'm pretty sure you ain't the one doing it."

"Mmm, thank you for that," she said dryly.

Cappy stood up. "What say we go pay Larry Proctor a little visit? Find out where he's been the last coupla hours."

"You think that will tell us anything?"

"Can't hurt."

Dennis rose too. "Well, I wish you good luck—"

"Hold it, Dennis," Cappy interrupted. "You're coming with us. I don't know about you yet and I'm not lettin' you out of my sight."

"But why?" Dennis protested. "I'd never even heard of Jordan McClure before tonight! I'm not involved in this!"

Mrs. McClure laughed shortly. "You're caught hiding in the laundry room of a man who's just been murdered and you say you're not involved? I think Cappy's right. You'd better come along."

Dennis made no further protest. He felt responsible for contributing to Jordan McClure's death . . . and Cappy was showing him his gun again. As the three of them left the house and made their way toward a gray sedan, Dennis remarked, "I must say, Mrs. McClure, you don't look very upset over your husband's death."

"Appearances can be deceiving," she answered. "As a matter of fact, I'm *very* upset that someone murdered him. I wanted to kill the bastard myself."

Cappy groaned. "Mrs. McClure, you shouldn't oughta say things like that. We don't know this guy here. He might think you really mean it."

"But I do really mean it. I've felt like killing Jordan for a *long* time. But I didn't. And I mean that, too."

Cappy handed her a set of keys and asked her to drive; he himself sat sideways in the front seat so he could keep an eye on Dennis in the back. "So, Dennis," Cappy drawled, "whaddaya do for a living?"

"I'm a C.P.A."

Cappy laughed. "The cooking accountant. Ever cook the books?"

Dennis was annoyed. "I'm a tax specialist."

"Well, Mr. Tax Specialist, you better pray Larry Proctor don't have no alibi. Because if he does, you're the only suspect we got to turn over to the police."

"Oh, then you are going to call in the police? That's heartening . . . I was beginning to wonder. Just when do you plan to let them in on what's happened?"

"Just as soon as I know for sure my client here ain't involved."

Mrs. McClure shot him a look that Dennis couldn't read.

Eventually they parked across the street from a brightly lighted white brick building; Dennis read the neon sign. "The Sagittarius Spa?"

"Larry usually comes by at this time to pick up his girl-friend Helga," Mrs. McClure explained. "She runs the place."

They found Larry watching Helga leading an exercise class. The music was bouncier than the customers were at that time of day. The women in the class were not the shapely young things seen in TV ads for workout videos; they were older, thicker, and hard-pressed to keep up with their energetic leader. Larry Proctor himself was rail-thin with a soulful puppy-dog face that probably brought out the mothering instinct in some women in spite of the fact that he was in his forties. He was so caught up in watching Helga that he didn't see them approach . . . and gave a yelp when Cappy dropped a heavy hand on his shoulder.

"Don't *do* that!" he exclaimed. "Oh . . . hello, Trish. What's up?" He shot a querulous glance at Dennis.

Trish McClure said, "Is there someplace private where we can talk, Larry?"

"Um, we could use Helga's office, I suppose. It's right down the hall." He made a few indecipherable hand gestures toward Helga while mouthing something; she smiled and nodded. Larry led the way.

The walls of Helga's office were covered with framed posters showing an assortment of healthy young people with perfect dentistry, all demonstrating various brands of exercise equipment. The décor of the room was remorselessly modern, and the only places to sit were on uncomfortable chairs that enforced good posture whether the sitter wanted it or not. Dennis decided to stand.

Larry Proctor asked, "What's this all about, Trish?"

But before she could answer, Cappy said, "Where you been the last coupla hours, Proctor?"

The skinny man winced at his aggressive tone but stood his ground. "Why do you want to know that, Mr. . . . Cappy, isn't it?"

"Yeah, I'm Cappy. Now quit stalling. Where you been?"

"Please, Larry," Trish McClure added, "it's important."

Larry shrugged. "I've been here for about twenty minutes. Before that, I was still at the office."

"Come off it, Proctor . . . it's nearly nine o'clock."

"So I worked late! So what? What's this all about?"

"How do you two know each other?" Dennis wondered aloud, meaning Larry and Cappy.

"Trish introduced us once," Larry said. "Who are you? And *what is going on?*"

Trish McClure told him. "Jordan was murdered tonight, Larry. He was shot."

His eyes bugged and his mouth dropped open . . . but

then he stopped moving altogether. *Frozen with shock, he is,* Dennis thought sympathetically.

That was the moment Helga made her entrance. In she burst, big and blond and muscled and sweaty. Dennis instinctively took a step backward. "Hello! Meeting is over, yes?" Helga hadn't yet adjusted down from shouting over the exercise music; her voice boomed through the office. She went to a small refrigerator and took out a pitcher filled with some bilious green liquid which she poured into a glass and handed to Larry. "Vitamins," she explained. "He needs building up."

Larry took the glass and drank mechanically, while Helga smiled broadly at the others, waiting for introductions that didn't come. The taste of the green concoction brought Larry out of his shock, but he finished the drink and put down the glass. When at last he spoke, it was to Dennis he turned. "Then you're the police?"

"No," Dennis answered, "I'm the unlucky stiff who found the body."

"Nice word choice there, Dennis," Cappy said.

Dennis's apology was drowned out by Helga's demanding to know what body; when Larry explained, she let loose a stream of Swedish and stalked out of the office. "She says we're not to leave until she showers and changes," Larry said.

Trish McClure stared at him. "I didn't know you understood Swedish."

"I don't. I just understand Helga."

Dennis was getting a headache.

Cappy picked up where he'd left off. "Anybody else in the office with you, Larry?"

"No, Jordan left . . . umm, around five-thirty."

Dennis nodded. "It was right after six when I saw him at

Cabot's Food Market. The man at the check-out counter can confirm that."

Trish looked at Cappy. "Is that right?"

"Yeah, yeah," Cappy said impatiently. "A little after six."

"Wait a minute," Dennis said. "You were there?"

"He was following Jordan," Trish said. "That's what I hired him to do."

"Then you saw me too," Dennis said to Cappy in a tone of outrage. "I stood there in front of the market talking to McClure a minute or two. And all this time you keep asking me who I am, where I come from—"

"I saw him talking to *somebody*," Cappy said testily. "I couldn't see your face . . . I was parked down the block. It coulda been anybody."

Dennis's sense of outrage collapsed. By six it was already pretty dark; Cappy probably couldn't make out his features from any distance. But then Dennis began to sweat. Cappy must have seen him pick up something from the sidewalk . . . but would he have been able to tell what it was? Or maybe he'd already left by then, following McClure. If he saw anything, he certainly wasn't saying so. Dennis was *very* uncomfortable.

But Cappy's attention was all on Larry Proctor. "So you got no alibi. You were alone, you say, from five-thirty to a half hour, forty-five minutes ago. Just during the time McClure got popped. Plenty of time to go from your office to McClure's house, shoot him, then come here and watch the ladies sweat. You coulda done it, Larry."

"Oh, don't be absurd. I'm not a killer. Why would I want to kill him anyway?"

"He was being blackmailed."

"*What?*"

"So maybe he gets tired of paying hush money," Cappy

improvised, "and decides to get rid of his blackmailer. But you're a little quicker—you get the drop on him. Pow! McClure's dead and you're off to the Sagittarius Spa to act innocent."

Dennis had never actually seen anyone tear his hair before. "This is insane!" Larry screeched. "I wasn't blackmailing him! And I didn't kill him!"

"Yeah? Now tell me another," Cappy said relentlessly.

Suddenly Trish stood up and started pacing. She stopped right in front of her husband's partner. "It's no good, Larry. I know Jordan caught you skimming."

That caught even Cappy by surprise. They all stared at the skinny man who had suddenly begun looking like a real murder suspect.

"Once! Just once!" Larry protested. "Jordan's been skimming off the top ever since we went into business together . . . and the one time I take a little something for myself—"

Trish said, "I heard him threaten to put you in jail."

"But I told him I'd put it back! I said I'd replace it!"

"Oh great, just what we need," Dennis muttered. "Another motive."

Larry attacked. "What about you, Trish? Jordan had the goods on you! I saw the evidence! You weren't going to get a cent out of that divorce!"

"Make that three motives," Cappy said.

Trish whirled on him and snapped, "You're supposed to be working for me!"

Cappy held up his hand in a *stop* gesture. "I ain't forgetting. But to the police, your motive is gonna look just as good as his."

"And we still have our unknown blackmailer, don't forget," Dennis said giddily.

"How do we know there's a blackmailer?" Larry asked.

25

Cappy looked pointedly at Trish. "Aha! We just have her word for it? That's all?"

"Why, you skinny little creep, how dare you?" Trish fumed. "Boy, was I wrong about you! You steal from the business, you kill my husband—"

"I didn't kill him! And don't pretend you're sorry he's dead, 'cause you're not!"

"I'm not pretending anything, you miserable little nudnik!" she screamed. "And if you think I'm going to let you—"

"Silence!"

Helga was back, showered and changed. Everyone obeyed her demand for silence. Trish walked away from Larry; both of them were obviously upset.

"I hear you all the way from locker room." Helga went over and wrapped an arm around Larry. "Poor baby. They give you hard time, huh?" She glowered at the others.

"There's something I don't understand," Dennis said. "Cappy, if you were following McClure, didn't you see whoever went into the house?"

"Naw, I left soon after he got home with his groceries. I called Mrs. McClure and she wanted to go see him, so I went to pick her up."

"My car's in the garage," Trish added.

"So that's when he was killed," Dennis mused. "While you were picking her up." *And while I was playing with his money.*

Larry was staring at Trish. "Then you couldn't have done it. Not if Cappy was watching him all the time until he came to get you. Oh Trish . . . I'm sorry!"

She waved a hand. "All right, all right."

Larry turned to Cappy. "But you could have done it. *Before* you went to get Trish."

"So could you, buddy-boy," Cappy answered testily. "And so could Dennis here. And even Helga, for all I know. The only one we've positively eliminated is Mrs. McClure."

There was a silence. Then Dennis asked, "So what do we do now?"

It was Helga who provided the answer. "We eat," she said firmly.

The restaurant booth wasn't large enough to accommodate five people, so Dennis and Trish took a second one. Dennis looked at the menu and groaned. Helga had brought them to a health-food place.

Trish smiled. "Not your kind of food?"

"Not even close. You know, I wouldn't be here now if I hadn't gone out to buy fresh basil."

"Enough to make you stick to canned goods, hmm?"

Dennis shuddered. "Never." He started telling her about the Sloshed Chicken.

In the next booth, Cappy complained, "I can't eat this rabbit food! I'm going out for burgers. Anyone want to come?"

No one did. Cappy left, and Dennis felt himself relaxing a little. Something about Cappy made him uneasy. "How'd you come to hire him?" he asked Trish.

"A friend recommended him. She said he'd gotten results for her in a similar situation."

"A similar situation. 'Domestic Cases Our Specialty.' "

"What a dumb euphemism." She sighed. "I committed a . . . an indiscretion. One time. Only once. What I didn't know was that Jordan was having me followed. His detective got pictures of us coming out of the motel, kissing goodbye, like that. You see, Jordan had a girlfriend. Hell, he had girlfriends all through our marriage. But he wanted to get rid of me so he could marry the latest one. So I hired Cappy to follow *him,* to get me some evidence so I wouldn't be totally defenseless when the divorce got really dirty."

"Did he find anything?"

She shook her head. "Whoever she is, she and Jordan were staying away from each other until the divorce was final. Jordan was a cheat in every sense of the word, but he wasn't stupid."

Dennis ordered and ate a sprouts quiche which somehow managed to have no taste to it whatsoever. "What did you want to see him about tonight?"

Trish said, "I was going to run a bluff. Tell him we did have evidence. I thought maybe with Cappy there looking tough and knowing, Jordan would get rattled enough to back off a bit."

"You think that would have worked?"

She looked so forlorn Dennis regretted asking the question. "Not really. But I couldn't think of anything else to try."

At that point Larry and Helga came over and joined them in their booth. "Helga has an idea," Larry said.

"Then let's hear it," Trish said. "I'm fresh out."

Helga announced, "We get rid of body."

"Good heavens!" Dennis exclaimed. "Why?"

"Because then Jordan McClure is merely one more Missing Person, no? They ask at airport, they show pictures at bus station. They do not ask us where we were during one hour of this day."

"Makes sense to me," Larry said. "If they don't know a time of death, how can they check alibis? We can weight the body down and sink it in the river. The only drawback, Trish, is that you'd have to wait seven years to have him declared legally dead. Can you hold out that long?"

"Without even breathing hard," she said quickly.

"But Trish," Dennis objected, "wouldn't it be to your financial advantage . . . having the body discovered now?"

"It would. But there's something that's worrying me." She took a deep breath. "Cappy. I don't really know him. And I can't think of any reason why he'd want Jordan dead. But suppose he did kill him right before he came to get me? Cappy is in my employ, remember. I could be charged with hiring him to kill Jordan."

They all digested that for a moment. "Cappy," Dennis murmured. "It always comes back to him."

Larry looked at his watch. "Speaking of, shouldn't he be back by now?"

"We go," Helga declared. "We go move body."

"How?" Dennis asked. "Cappy has the car."

They paid their bills and got back into their winter wraps, arguing about whether they should call a cab or not. "Cab drivers keep records of their fares," Larry objected. "It's a sure way to incriminate ourselves."

The problem was solved when Cappy drove up, chewing on a hamburger. The others piled in and told him Helga's plan.

Cappy didn't like it. "I could lose my license," he complained.

"Not if the police don't know about it," Trish pointed out. "It's the best way out for all of us, Cappy."

"Too many people in on this," he grumbled. "Somebody's bound to talk." He looked at Helga when he said it.

"I do nothing that hurts Larry," Helga insisted.

Eventually Cappy was persuaded. He drove them back to Jordan McClure's house and parked as far away from the street lamp as he could.

"Was this your house too?" Dennis asked Trish.

"No, that house is on the market. We both moved out."

The front door was closed but unlocked, the way they'd left it. They all moved reluctantly back to the kitchen.

The body was gone.

"That tears it!" Cappy said in disgust. "No body! We got another player, folks."

"The blackmailer?" Trish asked. "Why would he come back and take Jordan's body?"

"Maybe he had the same idea we did—missing person. I dunno."

Larry was staring at Cappy. "You must think we're really stupid. You disappear while we're eating, and when we get here—surprise, surprise! No body."

"Hey, wait a minute—"

"Did you think we wouldn't put the two together? Dumb move, Cappy."

The detective swore. "You guys are really itchin' to hang this on somebody, aren't you? But don'tcha need a little thing like motive? Why the hell would I want McClure dead?"

"Maybe you're the blackmailer," Dennis murmured, surprised at his nerve in suggesting it. "Maybe you killed in self-defense . . . if McClure was tired of paying you off and tried to get rid of you."

Cappy stared at him open-mouthed, speechless for once.

"I need a drink," Larry said.

"Alcohol, it poisons you," Helga admonished.

"Helga, love, this is an extraordinary situation we're all in here. I *need* a drink."

Trish found where McClure had kept his liquor and made drinks for all of them except Helga. They took their glasses and went to sit down in the living room.

"What is problem?" Helga asked. "Body is gone, yes?

30

Someone does our work for us."

Dennis was thinking back, trying to remember the one and only time he'd seen Jordan McClure alive. McClure had gotten into his car and driven away. A young couple had been on the street corner, arguing. A taxi had driven by and turned the corner. But only a taxi. There'd been no sound of another engine starting up, no car that had pulled away from the curb to follow McClure.

"Cappy," he said. "This is important. Tell us exactly what you saw when you were watching Cabot's Food Market."

"Why?"

"Please."

Cappy scowled, but did as Dennis asked. "I saw him come outside with his groceries. I saw him talk to somebody—you—for a few minutes. I saw him get in the car and drive away."

"And that's all you saw?"

"What else was there to see?"

"You didn't see a third man—the check-out counter man from Cabot's?"

Cappy's eyes narrowed. "Oh yeah—him. He came out too. What was that all about? Did McClure forget something?"

"Nice try, Cappy. You didn't see anything else? Just the three of us talking, and then McClure got in his car and drove away?"

Cappy swallowed visibly. "You gonna tell me there was a fourth man there too? That's bull."

The room was utterly devoid of sound, not even the clinking of ice in a glass. "McClure had a bad fall on the ice," Dennis said slowly. "His groceries were scattered all over the sidewalk. I picked them up. Louie—the check-out man—came running out to see if McClure was injured. But you saw none of that, Cappy. And you didn't see it, because you weren't there."

They were all waiting for an answer. None came. "Cappy?" Trish prompted.

He tried to carry it off. "Okay, so I didn't keep an eye on him *all* the time. Jeez, I knew he wasn't gonna do nothin' but buy groceries. So I didn't bother tailin' him. What's the big deal?"

"The big deal," Larry said, "is that you lied to us. What else have you lied about?"

"Maybe Cappy had stopped following him altogether," Dennis suggested. "Because maybe he'd already found what he wanted to know."

Cappy was sweating. "The name of Jordan's girlfriend?" Trish asked, appalled.

"And pictures, perhaps. The evidence you wanted, Trish. Wouldn't your husband pay to keep you from finding out?"

Trish rose slowly from her chair as a scream built in her throat. She lunged toward Cappy—but Helga was quickly on her feet, stopping Trish with a loose hammerlock around her waist. "Do not scratch eyes out," Helga instructed firmly. "We need him."

"All right, all right!" Cappy yelled. "So I was collecting a little something on the side! Yeah, I found McClure's popsie, but you woulda got the evidence before the divorce hearing, Mrs. McClure. Jeez, a guy's gotta make a living, don't he?"

"You son of a bitch," Larry said.

"But I didn't kill him!" Cappy insisted. "I wanted that guy alive! He was gonna pay me fifty thou later tonight. Mrs. McClure, you know what I thought when the two of us walked in here and found him dead on the kitchen floor? I thought, 'Shit, there goes my fifty thousand bucks.' That's what I thought. I'd be the *last* person to kill 'im!"

Helga asked, "You think of money when you see dead man?"

"Do you know something?" Dennis asked the room at large. "I believe him. I believe that's exactly what Cappy *would* think of."

Cappy didn't even see the insult. "At least one a youse is thinkin' straight."

Helga asked, "You move body?"

"Yeah, yeah. How'd I know you'd come up with the same idea?"

Then everyone fell silent, pondering this latest turn of events. After a couple of minutes had passed, Larry remarked, "Trish—you just lost your alibi. Since Cappy wasn't watching him all the time."

"Nah, she didn't do it," Cappy said. "I was on the phone to her a couple times during that hour when he was killed. She wouldna had time to make the round trip."

Larry nodded. "You just got it back again."

Dennis coughed gently to get their attention. "Cappy didn't kill him. Trish has been cleared. And I know damned well I didn't do it." He turned to Larry. "I'm afraid that leaves you."

Larry paled. "But . . . but I *didn't* kill him!"

"Foolish notion!" Helga scolded.

"Yeah," Cappy said, eager to finger someone else. "You had motive and opportunity. Just how much did you steal from the business, pal?"

Trish walked over to stand in front of Larry. "I think that's a fair question."

"Trish, I had already begun paying it back!" Larry pleaded. "Jordan gave me a time limit. If I could get it all returned in six weeks, he wouldn't turn me in."

Cappy sneered. "So you say."

"That doesn't sound like Jordan," Trish admitted. "He wasn't usually so generous."

"Maybe he was lying," Larry said desperately. "Maybe he was waiting until I paid back all the money and *then* he'd turn me in."

"*That* sounds like Jordan," Trish said.

"I don't care who it sounds like," Cappy said. "I think we found our murderer."

"This is crazy!"

"You're the only one left, Larry," Dennis repeated.

"And I know the two of you never really got along," Trish contributed.

"Make it easy on yourself, pal," Cappy added. "Tell us what happened."

"*ENOUGH!*" The voice that directed exercise classes commanded them to silence. "You leave Larry alone," Helga ordered. "I tell you truth now. I am one who shot Jordan McClure."

"Oh, Helga," Dennis said with a sigh. "Don't be silly."

"It is you who are silly. Over and over you say Larry is only one left. What about me?"

"You *want* to be a suspect? Helga, I know you're trying to protect Larry, but—"

"Hold it, hold it," Cappy interrupted. "Helga. Tell us what happened."

Dennis was irritated. Cappy was willing to believe anybody was guilty just so long as he was off the hook. But everyone was listening to what Helga had to say.

"I know what Jordan McClure wants to do to Larry," she stated. "I come here to this house, to tell him to leave Larry alone. He laughs at me. I get angry."

"Uh-oh," Larry said.

Helga nodded sadly. "It is not nice, when I get angry. Suddenly this man is pointing gun at me. At *me!*"

Cappy looked at Trish. "Did he own a gun?" She nodded. "Okay, Helga, what did you do?"

"Why, I take gun away from him!"

There wasn't a person in the room who doubted that she could do it. "Of course," said Dennis.

"Naturally," Trish echoed.

"But then he grabs big knife from drawer and comes straight at me," Helga went on. "So I shoot him."

"Right between the eyes," Dennis said. "Pow!"

Helga beamed. "Is good shot, no?"

Cappy half-groaned, half-laughed. "It was a fantastic shot. What did you do after you shot him?"

Helga raised her hands, palms up. "I go to spa and teach class."

That left everyone speechless except Larry, who was gazing admiringly at his protectress. "Isn't she terrific?"

Cappy was rubbing the back of his neck. "Jesus, Helga, that's a clear-cut case of self-defense if ever I heard one. Why didn't you just call the police?"

"And they believe me? They ask no questions, make no trouble? You are sure they do not send me to prison?"

"Not if you have a witness," Larry said stoutly. "I was here and saw the whole thing. What we do is, we put the body back in the kitchen and call the cops."

Cappy snorted. "You're her *boyfriend,* for Christ's sake. They're not gonna believe you."

"But they'll have to believe a second witness," Trish said. "I was here too."

Helga looked contrite. "I am sorry to make so much trouble," she said to Trish.

"Honey, you solved a big problem for me. It's the least I can do."

Dennis asked, "Are you sure you want to do this?"

Trish nodded.

"One problem," Cappy said. "The forensics guys are gonna know the body's been moved. How do you explain that?"

"With a modified version of the truth," Dennis suggested. "At first they thought about getting rid of the body and started to move it. Then they decided to make a clean breast of the whole thing and brought it back."

Cappy chewed that over. "Yeah, that'll do it. Let's make sure we got it straight. Helga tells how she shot him, exactly the way it happened. Larry and Mrs. McClure are her witnesses. And Dennis and me don't come into it at all."

"That's right," Trish said dryly. "You get off scot free."

"Not hardly," Cappy growled. "This evening cost me fifty thou, remember."

Helga asked Larry, "Do I owe him apology?"

"No," Larry said emphatically.

"Oh, Cappy," Dennis said. "Just one little teensy tiny thing. *Where's the body?*"

Cappy looked embarrassed. "It's in the trunk of the car."

"My god," Trish said. "You mean it was there all the time we were driving over here? Oh wow."

"Christ, I didn't have *time* to get rid of it! Jeez. Helga, where's the gun?"

"In garbage can. Next block."

"Go get it. Now." She took off running. Cappy turned to Dennis and said, "I could use some help. McClure was a big guy and rigor's set in."

Dennis's stomach turned over in distaste, but he went to help Cappy get McClure's corpse out of the trunk. "I can't believe I'm doing this," Dennis muttered as they worked the stiffened body out of the small space.

"Believe it, pal," Cappy panted.

Trish held doors open for them while Larry stood around helplessly flapping his hands. Helga came back with the gun.

When they finally had the scene in the kitchen set to everyone's satisfaction, Cappy said, "One final thing. If I'm gone and my car's gone, the cops are gonna wonder how you got here. Larry, you got wheels?"

"Yes."

"Then let's go get 'em. You drive the women back here and *then* call the police. Me and Dennis'll be long gone."

"Right! Glad you thought of that."

"Then let's go."

They'd reached the front door when Dennis held up one glove. "Oh . . . I must have left my other glove in the kitchen."

"For Christ's sake!" Cappy exploded. "Go find it. Hurry!"

Dennis ran back toward the kitchen but stepped into the laundry room first. He burrowed through the basket of dirty clothes until he found the billfold. Then he moved into the kitchen and slipped the billfold with its troublesome contents into Jordan McClure's pocket.

They were waiting for him in the car, the engine running. He slid into the backseat and shut the door, the evening's grocery-shopping finished at last.

SLOSHED CHICKEN

Chicken breasts (halved, skinned, and boned)
Bacon slices
Beer
Seasonings

Roll each chicken breast in one or more seasonings—basil, thyme, powdered bay leaf, rosemary (my favorite), arugula, tarragon, cilantro, whatever you prefer, even oregano. Coat thoroughly.

Wrap one bacon slice around each piece of chicken. Marinate in the beer 6-8 hours.

Bake at 350° for 30-35 minutes, basting frequently with beer. Serve with wild rice.

This story was written for the first Cat Crimes *anthology, before anyone knew the book would blossom into a successful series. The word "scat" is used in every meaning I could find for it—as in scat singer, in scatological jokes, as a slang term for heroin, and as in what you say to a cat you want to go away. The cat in this story is an exaggerated version of one of my own cats—a neurotic, chewed-upon, abandoned little animal named Daniel who was half-starved when he invited himself in to stay. Daniel took a full year to come to trust me, and I love him to death.*

SCAT

Tess fiddled with the adjustment band of her earphones; there ought to be some way to make the things stay up without the top part pressing so hard on her head. She was getting a headache.

An elbow jabbed her in the side. " 'Scuse me," said Pauline.

Tess grunted *okay.* She'd sung with Betty before, but Pauline was a stranger. The sound booth the three of them were crowded into was so tiny there was no room for stools to sit on. They'd been standing in there for nearly two hours, with only one break.

"Let's *go,*" Betty hissed.

The director must have heard her. "All right, girls," his voice said through their earphones, "let's try it again. Tess—

bright-voiced, happy. Betty and Pauline, remember—no *doo-wah. Ooh-ahh. Oooooh. Ahhhhh.* It's what the customers are supposed to say when they see the new Scimitar 2000. Ooh, ahh."

"Why do they keep naming cars after weapons?" Betty muttered.

"Ready?" said the director. "Here comes your count."

The three women listened to the metronomic ticking fed into their earphones from the control room. On the eighth beat the taped music came in. On the sixteenth beat, they began to sing.

"Be good to your-seh-helf," Tess started.

"Ooh-ahh, ooh-ahh."

"Only the best for you-hoo."

"Ooh-ahh, ooh-ahh."

"Hold it," the director's voice cut in. "Problem here." The earphones went dead. They could see him in the control room, yelling at the engineer who was trying to concentrate on the panel in front of him.

"Does this happen a lot?" Pauline asked.

"Yes," the other two said together.

They were all silent a moment, and then Betty said to Tess, "You look like hell. What time did you get in last night?"

"Four. God, I hate these morning sessions."

"Me too, and I was in bed by eleven."

Pauline looked as if she wanted to ask a question, but just then the director's voice told them they were ready to go again.

This time they got it, much to everyone's relief. Later the announcer's voice would be dubbed in, then the whole thing fitted to the visuals. If the timing was off by even two seconds, the singers would be called back to lay down a new track. Tess made a good living that way.

The director thanked them all effusively and promised their checks would be mailed out the next day. The three singers left together, knowing they'd done their part to help persuade the American viewing public that it was well worth risking bankruptcy to own a shiny new Scimitar 2000.

Tess turned down Betty's lunch invitation, waved goodbye, and headed for the lot where she'd left her car.

She was yawning by the time she unlocked her front door; five hours between gigs simply was not enough. She dragged into the kitchen and opened a can of soup. Almost as an afterthought she reached into the cabinet and pulled out a can of cat food. Ocean whitefish with tuna, oh yummy. "It's here if you want it," she called out.

Tess took her cup of steaming soup into the bedroom where she kicked off her shoes and eased onto the bed. Ooooh, that felt good, ahhh . . . and immediately she heard Betty's and Pauline's voices in her head singing *Ooh-ahh, ooh-ahh*. She laughed. What else could one do except laugh? Nobody liked singing crap for a living, but it paid the bills.

She finished most of the soup—beef barley—and rested the cup in her lap. She lay back against the big reading pillow and felt herself drifting toward sleep. Then a movement caught her eye. The cat was just inside her bedroom door, licking his paw and washing his face. It was the closest he ever came to thanking her for his food.

"Hello, Hugo," Tess said tiredly.

Hugo didn't answer. He was a small gray cat, with a broken tail and a chunk missing out of one ear. His coat was growing back in nicely, though. When Tess's sister had first brought him home, big patches of Hugo's fur were missing,

41

exposing ugly areas of raw, infected skin. One of his eyes had been sealed shut. And he'd walked with a limp.

Hugo had been a test animal in a cosmetics company's laboratory. God knew what they'd been trying out on him; but whatever it was, it had turned an ordinary alley cat into a vicious, semi-feral animal that saw every human gesture as a threat to his safety. Hugo had been rescued by PETA, the People for the Ethical Treatment of Animals, on one of their liberation raids. Tess's sister Debra, an ardent animal-rights activist, had been on that raid; Debra said they'd had to use a net to catch Hugo and drag him out. He'd fought and hissed and spit and clawed every inch of the way.

But then a couple of weeks later Debra learned she was being transferred to a new office her company was opening in Florida. It meant a promotion, and Debra had jumped at the chance. But uprooting the still maladjusted Hugo again so soon, at the same time she was house hunting and learning a new job . . . it was too much for her. Debra begged her sister to take Hugo; and in a moment of weakness, Tess had said yes. But Debra hadn't been completely honest about Hugo and his problems; all she'd said was, "Don't ever, *ever* try to stroke his back."

She hadn't told Tess that Hugo hated human beings—all human beings, no exceptions. At times it wasn't safe even to walk near him; the claws would lash out, ripping through cloth and skin. Yet even the one warning Debra had given her, Tess had managed to forget. On Hugo's first night with Tess, it had seemed the most natural thing in the world to stretch out her hand for a little cat-petting. Hugo had sunk his teeth into the back of her hand all the way down to the bone. She still bore the scars that little gesture of friendliness had cost her.

A light thump on the end of the bed startled Tess; Hugo

sat crouched there, eyeing her suspiciously, ready to pounce at the first sign of danger. It was the only time he'd ventured onto the bed in the six months he'd been living with her. His eyes left hers and traveled to the cup in her lap.

Ah, it was the remains of the soup he wanted. "Still hungry, are you? It's all right, Hugo," she said soothingly as she moved the cup slowly toward him. "You can have it if you want." She drew back her hand and waited.

Eventually Hugo decided no trap was lying in wait and crept up to the cup. He finished the soup and licked the inside of the cup.

Tess smiled. "You like that, huh?" Her eyes slowly closed. She was almost asleep when she felt the lightest of pressures on her stomach. It felt like a cat paw.

She opened one eye. Hugo was testing her stomach while watching warily for any sign of reaction. Tess lay as still as she could, one arm draped across her waist. Taking his time, the cat oozed up onto her stomach and made himself comfortable. Hugo wasn't very heavy but he was warm; he felt good there. Tess was almost ecstatically pleased at this miraculous turn of events.

But the miracles weren't over yet. After a few minutes Hugo started nudging at her hand with his nose, gently, repeatedly. *He wants to be petted?* Tess wondered. Hesitantly she touched his head with the tips of her fingers; Hugo moved into the caress. To her surprise Tess found he liked to have his face stroked. A low rumbling noise began. It was the first time she'd ever heard him purr.

Breakthrough! Breakthrough! Tess grinned foolishly at the thought of falling asleep with a cat purring on her stomach. Especially this cat. It was true, a little love and kindness could—

But then she became aware the purring had stopped.

Hugo was staring at her, making that kind of hypnotic eye contact only cats can manage. Hugo's own eyes were in what Tess thought of as his "attack mode." She pulled back her hand . . . but not fast enough. Hugo lashed out, his claws catching the side of her hand. Tess yelped with the pain; Hugo thumped down off the bed and disappeared.

"You stupid cat!" Tess yelled. "*I'm* not the one who hurt you!"

The pain was shooting all the way up her forearm. She went to the bathroom for antiseptic and a couple of Tylenol before returning to bed and trying to think herself into the proper frame of mind for sleep.

The Corner Bar wasn't on a corner and it was trying to be more than just a bar. It was located in a neighborhood of slum buildings and half-hearted restorations, nearly all the street-level space taken up by pawnshops, dry cleaners, cheap furniture stores, appliance outlets, greasy spoons. A small-time entrepreneur named Phil Maynard had bought the Corner Bar when it was a failing comedy club and was doing his best to turn it into a jazz spot. But there were problems.

The four-piece band was doing a set when Tess slipped in the back way. Lazy jazz, too early in the evening for anything else. Tess stood at a beaded curtain in a doorway and peeked out at the "stage"—just a small raised platform at one end of the room. The bass player had hair so blond it was almost white; he stared vacantly into space, his pupils jumping. Only nine-thirty and already flying. The other three members of the band, all black, were laughing at him. Tess suspected they laughed at her too; a black customer had once told her bluntly *White meat can't scat.* But Lester, the piano man, could follow anything she did. They got along.

"I want you to split your set tonight, Tess," a voice said in her ear. "Half before Tommy, half after."

She turned angrily; Phil Maynard, a beefy man with wiry black hair, was staring over her shoulder at the small audience. "That's a helluva thing to do to me, Phil! Why?"

He nodded toward the audience. "Joey LaCosta."

Oh. Tess's heart sank. LaCosta was an insider—they didn't like to be called "wiseguys" anymore—and everyone who knew him was afraid of him. Tess picked him out in the audience, sitting at a center table with two of his troopers. LaCosta had started dropping in to listen to Tommy Vincenza, an unsuccessful stand-up left over from the days when the bar was trying to make it as a comedy club. Tommy specialized in bathroom jokes. All of his jokes were old ones, and most of them weren't even funny. But Joey LaCosta liked Tommy's scatological humor; and what Joey liked, Joey got. When LaCosta had oh-so-politely mentioned that clinking glasses distracted him, Phil had got the message and stopped serving drinks while Tommy was on.

LaCosta didn't want to hear Tess; he'd put up with a little scat-singing while waiting for his man, but not a whole lot. "I'll split my set," Tess muttered.

"See those two guys over to the left by the wall?" Phil asked. "Cops."

Tess looked at them. "How can you tell?"

"I know one of 'em." He growled. "I try to run a nice clean club here and what do I get? Crooks and cops. I wouldn't have none of 'em if it wasn't for Tommy, but I can't get rid of him or LaCosta'll start leanin' on me." He rubbed a big hand across his mouth. "I'm gonna have to fire that bass player. Cops look at him and think we're sellin' drugs here and we're all in deep shit."

"Is that why they're here? They think—"

"Naw, they're keepin' an eye on LaCosta. Go get changed, Tess. Let's get rollin'.'"

"Why don't you put Tommy on now and let me do my set after?"

"Tommy ain't here yet. Go on, Tess."

She went to the communal dressing room, a small ex-storeroom to which a few mirrors and tables had been added. Tess climbed up on a chair to reach the gown she'd left hanging on the exposed water pipe that ran through the room. It was the same gown she'd worn the night before, but it didn't matter; the Corner Bar didn't attract the kind of customers that came back night after night.

And that too was Tommy Vincenza's doing. Music lovers would drop in for a little listening; but when Tommy got into his routine, always, every night, some of the customers would get up and wander out. Tommy turned people off. He was a throwback; people had stopped laughing at Tommy's kind of toilet humor years ago. All except Joey LaCosta. Joey LaCosta thought Tommy was a riot.

Tess had finished dressing and was fixing her make-up when Tommy walked in, carrying a blue airline bag. He was short, coming up only to Tess's shoulder, and almost as round as he was tall. A sixtyish man, Tommy had the bleary eyes and red-veined nose of a lifelong serious drinker; but his speech never seemed to be affected no matter how much alcohol he consumed. Before sitting down or saying hello, he pulled a bottle out of the airline bag, poured himself a shot, and downed it.

"Ah, that's better." He turned a bloodshot eye toward Tess and gave her a lopsided smile. "You're looking fetching tonight, m'dear!"

"Aren't you a little early, Tommy?"

"Yeah, I thought I might as well come on in. Didn't have

anything else to do. Hey, Tessie, did you hear this one? How is the starship *Enterprise* like a roll of toilet paper?"

"I don't want to hear," she said firmly.

"They both circle Uranus and search for Klingons."

She just looked at him. And then changed the subject: "Did you know your number-one fan is here?"

"Mr. LaCosta, yes. Phil told me."

"You don't mind playing to the mob?"

"Mind? When Mr. La Costa laughs, everybody laughs. I don't mind that at all."

"Then you don't want to keep him waiting, do you? Why not do your routine first tonight?"

"Ah, m'dear, it's not that easy. You need to assimilate a certain amount of anaesthetic before you can go out and wipe the Mafia's ass." He poured another shot.

Tess gave up. She went and stood by the doorway with the beaded curtain until Phil was ready to introduce her. By then the customers had built up a good cloud of cigarette smoke. By midnight the haze would be so thick she'd have trouble breathing; not the best of conditions for a singer.

Phil went through his usual rigmarole of welcoming everyone, promising them *qrrrreat!* entertainment and so on. "And now here she is," he finished, "the Corner Bar's own—Tess Ridgeway!"

A polite smattering of applause greeted her entrance. She glanced at the piano player and said, "Only half a set, Lester." Lester nodded, as if expecting something like that.

She might as well have been singing Greek folk songs for all the attention the audience paid. The two cops by the wall kept their eyes on Joey LaCosta. LaCosta was telling a story to his two troopers, a story that required much waving of the hands. The other customers were either listening to him openly or sneaking glances in his direction; an underworld celebrity was still a celebrity. The bar's one waitress moved among the tables, taking orders, delivering drinks. By the time Tess had gotten a few of the customers listening to her, her half-set was over.

Lester rolled his eyes in sympathy as the band members prepared to leave the stage. Tess charged off, snarled something at Tommy waiting to go on, and slammed into the dressing room.

A minute later the dressing room door opened and Cheryl, the waitress, came in carrying a drink. "Thought you could use this," she said with a friendly smile.

"Thanks, Cheryl." It was scotch, and it went down smoothly, caressing Tess's throat instead of burning; Cheryl had dipped into Phil's good stock. Tess grinned. "*Thanks, Cheryl!*"

Cheryl laughed and patted her blond frizz. "Tommy's feeling no pain. First time I ever saw him weave." She'd left the dressing room door open, and both women could hear LaCosta's *haw-haw-haw* booming out from the audience. "That must have been an especially gross one."

Tess took another swallow of the scotch. "If I were Phil," she said, "I'd buy Tommy a plane ticket to Los Angeles and then tell LaCosta he'd gotten an offer to go on TV."

Cheryl nodded. "That might do it. But Tommy could always come back."

"Yeah," Tess said glumly.

Both women were silent a minute . . . and then it hit them that the audience was equally silent. No applause, no Mafiaesque guffaws, nothing. Uneasy, Tess put down her drink. She and Cheryl stepped out of the dressing room to see what was going on.

They found Phil standing by the beaded curtain, staring out at Tommy, a look of horror on his face. "Is he out of his mind?" he asked. "Is the little twerp *out of his fuckin' mind?*"

Out on the stage, Tommy was sweating, playing to his one-man audience and straining for the laughs that just weren't coming. "There was a cop who was taking this wiseguy in for questioning."

Tess and Cheryl gasped.

"On the way they pass this little kid playing with a pile of shit. The cop says, 'Yucch, that's disgusting! What are you doing with that shit?' And the kid says, 'I'm making a cop.' The wiseguy thinks that's funny but the cop gets mad. So the cop says, 'That's terrible, why are you making a cop out of shit?' And the little kid says, 'Because I don't have enough for a wiseguy.' "

"*Jeeeeeesus,*" Phil groaned. Out front—dead silence.

Tommy tried again. "Two other wiseguys, they're worrying about another member of the family, a cousin who walks with a kind of swish? So one day they follow him, and sure enough the cousin leads them straight to a gay bar. They watch as he looks over the action and finally picks out a comely-looking lad sitting at the bar. The cousin goes up to stand behind the lad and he says, 'Hi, there—mind if I push in your stool?' "

That did it. *"Basta!"* Joey LaCosta jumped out of his chair and pointed a finger at Tommy. "Who you think you are, you shit-for-brains? Hanh?" No one made a sound as LaCosta charged toward the now-trembling comic. "You stand up here and you make fun of my family? *My* family?"

"Mr. LaCosta, I—"

"I come to this shitty little club, I listen to you, I laugh at your jokes. I even slip you a nice tip now and then. And what do you do? You stand up here and mock me! You mock my family, you mock my business—what kind of way is that to show respect?"

"But Mr. LaCosta, I only—"

"You only what? I'll tell you what you only. You only insulted me, that's what you only. You insulted me in public."

"Oh no, that wasn't what I meant—"

"*Shaddup.* I'm thinking." LaCosta's two bodyguards moved up to flank him, in case he needed help in handling the dangerous Tommy Vincenza. Finally LaCosta said, "Awright. Here's what I decided. You gave me a lotta good laughs, Tommy, so I'm not going to do nothing this time. But if I ever hear you been telling these kinda jokes again, you know what's gonna happen, don't you? You hear me, Tommy? You hear what I'm saying to you?"

Tommy's voice came out in a squeak. "I hear you, Mr. LaCosta. But believe me, please, I meant no disrespect! I didn't mean anything by it!" He was talking to LaCosta's retreating back. "I thought you'd be pleased!" he called in one last attempt to mollify his former patron.

The three mobsters left; one of the cops got up and followed them. Phil ran out and dragged Tommy off the stage. Both men were panting. "Jesus Christ, Tommy, what's the matter with you?" Phil said to the quivering comic. "You got some kind of death wish or something?"

"Yeah, Tommy," Cheryl said, wide-eyed, "that was pretty dumb even for you!"

The comic looked so frightened and confused that Tess felt sorry for him. "But, but he said Mr. LaCosta *liked* jokes about the mob!" Tommy whimpered.

"Who said?"

"One of his boys. One of those guys here with him tonight."

Phil was thunderstruck. "And you believed him? You actually *believed* him?"

"Well, why would he tell me that if—"

"Because he was tired of coming in here. Because he wanted to make trouble. Because he was bored. Who the hell knows why? Jesus Christ, Tommy, how could you be so stupid? If you've brought the mob down on me, I swear to god I'll—"

"You can't fire me!" Tommy screeched. "You know you can't fire me!"

Phil stopped short. He licked his lips but said nothing.

"Wow," Tess said, "that must be some contract you have, Tommy. Who's your agent?"

Tommy was breathing heavily. "No contract. Phil and me don't need no contract. Do we, Phil?"

Just then the four band members came in from the alley where they went between sets to get away for a while. Lester took in the picture in one glance and muttered, "Back outside."

"No, hold it," Phil commanded. "Go out there and play—*now*. Something lively, get their minds off what just happened. Go on, move!"

Not one of the band members asked what did happen; they crowded past Tess and Cheryl single file through the beaded curtain.

Tommy had had time to think about LaCosta's threat. "J-Jeez, Phil," he stammered, "wh-what am I going to do?"

"I'll tell you what you're goin' to do." Hands on hips, Phil glowered down at the little man. "Right now, you get the hell out of here. Then tomorrow you go to LaCosta and you apologize. Then you tell him exactly what you told me. You finger the goon, make trouble for *him*. And Tommy— don't come back here until you do it."

"You can't fire me!"

"I'm not firing you, I just don't want you out on that stage until this business is settled. Y'unnerstand?" Tommy nodded. "All right, then, beat it." The comic dragged away, his shoulders slumping.

Tess stared at Phil, amazed that he was willing to let the comic come back at all. "Tommy must have something on you."

His face turned red. "Mind your own goddamned business. Get out there and do somethin', help 'em out." He turned to glare at Cheryl. "Why aren't you takin' orders?" Cheryl ducked her head and hurried away. Phil looked back at Tess. "I thought I told you to go sing!" He pushed her through the beaded curtain.

The customers were still buzzing about the incident and not paying the slightest attention to the entertainers. Tess looked at Lester and shrugged. He shrugged back and played a couple of chords on the piano. Tess sang a few nonsense syllables, no particular song. He hit another chord, she sang *dah-doo-dah-diddley*. This went on for a minute or two; finally the crowd began to quiet down. Tess slid into *Icehouse Blues*.

Then something magical began to happen. Tess found her true voice and started singing the way she wished she could sing all the time. She built slowly, moving from slow song to less slow, picking up the tempo and pacing herself until the customers were yelling *Yeah!* at the end of each number. One part of scat singing was trying to reproduce the sound and phrasing of musical instruments; the brasses were easy, but this night Tess found she could actually do the wail of a saxophone. Occasionally she'd yield to one of the band members, dah-doo-diddling along in harmony as each one did his turn; even the blond hophead on bass had his inspired moment. Then came the climax of the set, and Tess threw back her head and gave it her all. She felt great; for one solid hour she'd been wrapped up in the kind of joy that came only from doing what she loved best and doing it well.

"Not bad, Babe," Lester said when she'd finished. It was the first compliment he'd ever paid her.

Offstage, a laughing Phil gave her a big hug. Cheryl was there too, excited and holding out a drink that Tess didn't need this time. But she took it anyway, thanked them both, and headed for the dressing room.

She was pacing in the cramped little room, trying to walk off her adrenaline high, when a knock came at the door. It was the cop who'd stayed after LaCosta had walked out.

"Hi, I don't want to disturb you," he said, smiling, "but I just had to tell you that was the absolutely best scat singing I have ever heard."

She said thank-you and then laughed. "And how many scat singers have you heard?"

He grinned back at her. "Only three or four. You're not exactly mainstream, you know."

"I know. For most people, scat's a nostalgia thing. But it'll never die out completely. It's too much fun."

"Still, if you can earn a living at it—"

Tess made a face. "Nobody can live on what Phil Maynard pays. I have another job. You know those voices singing away in the background of TV commercials? Sometimes that's me."

He hesitated and then said, "I haven't introduced myself. My name's Graham Burke."

Tess nodded. "Pleased to meet you, Graham." She waved her glass in the air. "I'd like to offer you a drink, but this is all I've got."

"That's all right, I'm on duty anyway. I'm a police detective."

"I know. Why did you stay behind when your partner followed our visiting mobsters out?"

"He'll contact me if he needs me," Graham Burke said shortly. "Tell me, how did you get started in this kind of singing?" Big smile.

Warning bell; he hadn't answered her question. "You're watching someone here, aren't you?" she guessed.

The smile disappeared. "I can't talk about that."

"Which means yes."

An awkward pause developed. "Well, thanks again for some great singing." He smiled wryly and left.

Tess's good feeling had vanished. The police were keeping the Corner Bar under surveillance. Immediately she thought of the coked-up bass player—but why hadn't they just arrested him, if drugs were what they were looking for? Could LaCosta have some connection with the club other than Tommy Vincenza? Then she remembered that Tommy had something on Phil, something strong enough to force him to keep Tommy on the payroll even though the comic attracted the kind of customer Phil wanted to avoid. Phil? The police were keeping an eye on Phil?

With an effort she put it all out of her mind. She had two more sets to get through, and it would take some doing to match the pitch and intensity of the last one. Tess had to conserve her energy; it would be hours before she could climb on the chair to hang her gown on the water pipe and go home to Hugo.

Tess slept until noon and got up then only because Hugo was scheduled to get his shots at two. The cat was prowling about and hissing, mad because she wouldn't let him out. Tess stayed out of his way.

She should never have let him become an outside cat in the first place. One day she'd caught him shredding her living room drapes with his claws. She'd opened the door and yelled *Scat!* and chased him out, secretly hoping he'd run away. But no such luck; Hugo kept coming back to the one place in the world where he could count on a safe place to sleep and something to eat.

One of Tess's dates had tried to pet Hugo when she wasn't looking; Hugo had bitten and scratched so violently that she'd had to drive the man to the emergency room of the nearest hospital for treatment. The doctor told her to get the cat declawed; Tess said that would leave him defenseless out of doors. Her date had been more blunt: *Have him put away.* Hugo was not a pet, he pointed out; he was a savage creature that she was foolishly harboring and that would one day turn against her.

But Tess couldn't bring herself to have the cat destroyed. Instead, she'd called the ASPCA. They told her they'd take Hugo, but he'd probably be put to sleep; people wanted to adopt kittens, not cats. So then she asked the vet who treated Hugo to help find him a new home. Dr. McInerny had been politely discouraging, saying he couldn't in good conscience foist Hugo off on anyone.

So she was stuck. Tess was just going to have to put up with him and pray that sooner or later he'd come around.

She started getting ready to take Hugo to Dr. Mc-Inerny's office. An Ella Fitzgerald tape was playing, buoying Tess up a little; Ella always made it sound so easy. Tess took the portable kennel out of the closet, being careful to close the bedroom door so Hugo wouldn't see it just yet. Hugo hated the kennel; he hated to ride in a car, he hated being taken to a different place, he hated all those dangerous humans in the vet's office. Sighing with resignation, Tess got out a pair of welder's mitts that came all the way up to her elbows; she always hated this part.

It was a battle. But no matter how fiercely Hugo bit and clawed at the protective mitts, Tess held on and finally got him into the kennel. The first obstacle was over. Tess turned off Ella Fitzgerald and carried Hugo to the car.

He yowled all the way. Inside the vet's office, he switched to a low menacing growl, ready to take on anything that moved. The assistant was ready for him, though; she was wearing animal handler's gloves when she took Hugo out and held him on the examination table.

"Don't touch his back," Tess reminded Dr. McInerny.

"I remember," he said. Swiftly he gathered up the fur over Hugo's collarbone, inserted the needle, and it was done. "Do you know how male lions kill each other?" Dr. McInerny asked as his assistant wrestled the spitting, scratching cat back into the kennel. "They kill each other with a bite to the spinal cord. Hugo still feels threatened by what the experimenters did to him and he's literally watching his back. We don't know his full history—it could be a long time before he comes to trust you."

"So be patient?" Tess asked wryly.

"So be patient."

On the ride back Hugo didn't make a sound. He crouched into a small ball and stared out of the kennel, never taking his eyes off Tess. At home he didn't run away and hide as he usually did but instead stayed close to Tess, following her from room to room. When she plopped down to read the paper, he sat on her feet. He looked so small and vulnerable huddled there that her heart went out to him. When later she went into the kitchen, he went with her, staying underfoot all the time. When she sat at the table to eat, there was Hugo, sitting on her feet again.

Then she got it. He was *anchoring* her there, trying to keep her from going away, from abandoning him.

"Oh, Hugo," Tess said with a sigh. "Whatever am I going to do with you?"

That night Tess found Phil behind the bar, grinning and pouring a drink for Tommy, who looked happier than she'd ever seen him. She perched on the bar stool next to the comic and said, "You must have patched things up with your pal Joey."

Tommy raised his right hand with two fingers crossed. "We're like that, m'dear, we're like that."

"Tommy told him about the goon who caused all the trouble," Phil said.

"He believed you?" Tess asked Tommy.

"He sure as hell did! This trooper—his name's Alfio—seems like he'd given Mr. LaCosta grief before. Mr. LaCosta said, 'Alfio, I told you the last time, if you pulled any more stunts I was gonna have you sweeping the floor of one of our factories!' He went on talking like that—like I wasn't even there listening! Then he told Alfio to get the hell out and he'd deal with him later."

"Well, hallelujah," Tess said with a smile.

"Yeah, ain't it great?" Phil looked pleased, but Tess thought he must be of two minds about this turn of events. Happy that the mobsters were no longer mad, not so happy that they'd be coming back to the Corner Bar.

"And Tessie, you know what he did next?" Tommy said with a note of awe in his voice. "He apologized to me! Joey LaCosta apologized to *me!* And he gave me this." He showed her his left hand, a ring glittering on his little finger. "I never had a pinkie ring before in my life," Tommy said in that same tone of awe. "Those are real rubies, you know. Took it right off his own hand and gave it to me."

Tess shook her head but didn't say anything; Tommy's

gangster-worship could lead to no good end. Cheryl came up to the bar to get an order filled and Tess asked her, "How are they tonight?" Meaning the customers.

"Lethargic, kind of," Cheryl said. "I don't think these are the same people who were here before. I mean, I don't remember these faces. Nobody from last night."

"Probably afraid of an encore."

"Wouldn't you be?"

Tess looked over the small crowd. Not much talk going on; most of the customers were just sitting staring into their glasses. An unusual number of solitary drinkers, some of whom looked as if getting blind raging drunk within the next few hours was the only goal in life worth pursuing. Lester and the other band members came straggling out and started getting ready to play. "At least we won't have to worry about LaCosta again for a while."

"Oh, didn't I tell you?" Tommy interposed, still admiring his ruby ring. "Mr. LaCosta's coming back again tonight. To show there are no hard feelings, he said."

Tess and Cheryl exchanged a look. "Wonderful," Phil said tonelessly.

Tommy was feeling good, his bleary eyes more open than Tess had ever seen them. "Say, girls, did you hear the one about the—"

"I've got to go change," Tess said quickly and slipped away from the bar.

"A customer wants me," Cheryl announced and darted off.

Ah well, Tess thought as she made her way back to the dressing room, *he still has Phil to listen to him.*

Poor Phil.

Halfway through Tess's set, Joey LaCosta and his two

shadows came in. One of the two had been there the night before, but the other was a new face, a replacement for the troublemaking Alfio.

The mood of the crowd had changed. Friday was always the Corner Bar's best night, and the lethargy that characterized the early drinkers had disappeared altogether. The customers were talking cheerfully, drinking, even listening to Tess. Graham Burke and his partner were sitting at their same table by the wall; Tess hadn't noticed them come in. She was singing only peppy songs, since that seemed to fit the mood of the crowd, and the band was bouncing right along with her. Cheryl was busy, even looking a little harried; Phil ought to think about bringing in extra help on the weekends. When Tess finished her set to noisy, good-natured applause, she threw Graham a wink; he responded with a smile and a wave.

When she pushed through the beaded curtain, she was surprised to find Tommy wasn't waiting to go on. Phil usually introduced the comic, but tonight he was out front pouring drinks as fast as he could. The band members started coming off the stage for their break. "Tommy's not here," she said to Lester.

"Dressing room," he mumbled and headed straight for the alley.

"All right, *don't* help me look for him!"

He didn't. None of the band did. They were in too big a hurry to get to the alley and do whatever they did there between sets.

Muttering to herself, Tess made her way to the dressing room. The door was closed, generally a sign that someone was changing clothes. She pounded on the door with her fist. "Tommy! You're on."

No answer.

"Come on, Tommy! They're waiting." She opened the door and drew back as an unexpected stench made her gag. She pushed the door the rest of the way open . . . and found Tommy.

He was hanging by the neck from the water pipe that ran through the dressing room, the rope knotted high under his right ear. As if in a trance Tess moved toward him, drawn by the strangeness and unbelievableness of what she'd walked in on. She saw the comic's hands had been tied behind his back. As if hypnotized she stared at his hands, eventually realizing that his briefly-owned but highly-prized pinkie ring was missing. Finally the smell drove her back; in his last moment of life, Tommy had fouled himself.

Outside, she closed the dressing room door and leaned against it, a tightness in her chest making it hard to breathe. Then, without warning, a surge of fear swept over her. Someone who killed people was *here,* right here. Right now.

She ran out front as fast as she could and screamed at Detective Graham Burke that Tommy Vincenza had been murdered.

A Lt. Iverson had arrived to take charge of the case, which should have warned Tess right there: police lieutenants normally did not investigate personally the slayings of third-rate comedians in low-rent night spots. Graham Burke had dashed after Tess following her startling announcement, while the Corner Bar's customers all suddenly remembered appointments they had elsewhere. Graham's partner had had the presence of mind to restrain Joey LaCosta, which meant his two troopers had stayed behind as well.

Lt. Iverson—balding with protruding eyes and big teeth—could be the kindly uncle or the threatening authority figure, whichever the occasion called for. He'd huddled with Graham when he first arrived and put off asking questions until the Crime Scene Unit had arrived and completed the search for physical evidence. Taking pictures, dusting for prints, putting things in little plastic bags. Finally Tommy's body was cut down and carried away in a body bag. Only then did the tightness in Tess's chest begin to ease.

Graham stopped by the table where she was sitting with Cheryl and placed a hand on her shoulder. "You holding up all right?" She nodded. "The Lieutenant wants you to tell him about how you happened to find Tommy. He'll be over in a minute." She nodded again.

The customers' mass exodus had narrowed down the number of suspects considerably. They sat at the tables between the bar and the stage—Tess, Cheryl, Phil, the four band members, and Joey LaCosta with his two ever-present musclemen. Right behind LaCosta in a posture of guardianship stood Graham's partner, a fair-haired man named Stefanovich. A number of uniformed officers were still present. Lt. Iverson looked as if he wanted to make a speech but settled for walking over to Tess and Cheryl's table. "Which of you is Tess Ridgeway?" he asked.

"I am."

He sat down opposite her. "I'm sorry to put you through this, Ms. Ridgeway," the kindly uncle said, "but I want you to tell me how you came to find the body."

Tess told him. She told how Tommy had not been waiting to go on as usual and she'd gone to the dressing room to get him and found him dead. She mentioned the missing ruby ring. She said she didn't touch anything but came straight out front and told Graham Burke.

Graham's partner, Stefanovich, cleared his throat. "She told everybody else as well," he said. "She just shrieked it out."

Tess glared at him. "I do not *shriek*."

Iverson raised his eyebrows. "That's when all the customers took off? Yes. Where was the band during all this?"

"Out in the alley."

"In the alley? Really." He turned to face the band members, each of whom was sitting at a different table. "What were you doing in the alley, fellows?"

"Breathin'," Lester muttered.

"Oh my, we got a wisemouth here. Now listen—"

"No, man, that's what we were doin'—breathin'," Lester insisted. "Gets mighty smoky in here."

"Isn't that the truth," Cheryl said with a nod.

The police lieutenant looked unconvinced but didn't pursue it. "When did you last see the victim, Ms. Ridgeway?"

"Oh . . . it was right before I went to get changed. He was showing me his ring. Lieutenant, this wasn't just an ordinary robbery, was it?"

"Not a chance. The killer didn't even try to make it look like a robbery—the ring must have been an afterthought." He turned and addressed the room at large. "Who was the last to see Tommy?"

There was a silence, and then Phil said, "I guess I was. He was sittin' here at the bar until Tess started her set, then he went back to the dressing room."

"Did you see him go into the dressing room?"

"Well, no, I was behind the bar."

At that moment Joey LaCosta heaved a much-put-upon sigh. "Lieutenant, how long am I gonna have to sit here listening to this?"

The kindly uncle changed into the authority figure. "Until I'm satisfied you had nothing to do with this killing.

And LaCosta—I'm not easily satisfied."

"Why would I kill the guy? I liked him!"

"When was the last time you saw him?"

"I didn't see him at all tonight. Tommy never came on 'til the bird finished singing."

Chirp chirp, Tess thought.

Iverson turned back to Phil. "Had Tommy already gone back to the dressing room by the time LaCosta got here?"

Phil thought back. "Yeah, he had."

"That's right, Lieutenant," Stefanovich interposed. "Me and Burke, we were right behind LaCosta. Tommy wasn't out here."

Iverson nodded, clear at last on the sequence of events. "We're going to take your statements individually now. Mr. Maynard, I'd like to use your office."

Phil shrugged. "Sure."

"Lieutenant," Tess said, "are you finished with the dressing room yet? My street clothes are in there, and . . ." She gestured to the sparkly gown she was wearing.

"We're not quite finished, but—Burke, do we have any female officers on the premises?"

"I'll see." Graham left and returned almost immediately with a short black woman. "This is Officer Dodson."

Iverson said, "Dodson, go with Ms. Ridgeway while she changes her clothes. Make sure she touches nothing other than her personal belongings."

"Yessir." Officer Dodson followed Tess out of the room.

But when Tess got to the dressing room, she hesitated.

"The body's been removed," the policewoman said gently.

"I know. I still don't want to go in there." But she made herself do it.

Tommy's last stench lingered slightly; the dressing room

had no windows for airing the place out. Tess slipped out of her gown and decided to take it home rather than hang it back up on the water pipe. She put on jeans and sneakers and was pulling a sweater over her head when the door banged open and two cops walked in.

"Hey!" yelled Officer Dodson. "Knock first!"

"It's all right, I'm ready," said Tess. She gathered up her gown, her raincoat, her purse.

"Sorry," said one of the cops, as they both set about their business—business that was noticeably different from the careful, even finicky approach taken by the Crime Scene Unit. These two looked under tables, pulled out drawers and checked behind them, shone a light in the ventilator shaft.

"What are you looking for?" Tess asked.

"Scat."

"What?" Indignantly.

Officer Dodson explained. "Scat. Heroin. Wanna play word association? Joey LaCosta, scat."

"But, but he wouldn't have any heroin stashed here," Tess objected as she and the policewoman left the dressing room. "The Corner Bar's not part of LaCosta's operation. The only reason he ever came here was to listen to Tommy." *Which he wouldn't be doing anymore,* she suddenly thought. Probably the only good thing to come out of the comic's death.

"Still gotta check," the black woman said. "LaCosta's got a partner we can't finger, and LaCosta keeps coming back to the Corner Bar."

"That's why the police have been watching the place?"

"C'mon, let's go. My sergeant says I talk too much."

It was more than an hour before the police got around to taking Tess's statement. By then all four members of the band had left. Phil and Cheryl were straightening the place up, Phil washing glasses as fast as Cheryl could carry them from the deserted tables. Lt. Iverson and Graham were drinking coffee that Phil had made for them, letting Stefanovich take a crack at LaCosta in Phil's office. LaCosta's two bodyguards were gone, ordered by the police to wait outside.

Lt. Iverson stood up when he saw Tess coming, back to the kindly uncle again. He smiled, showing his big teeth, and pulled a chair out from the table. "Ms. Ridgeway?"

"I'm awfully tired, Lieutenant," Tess said. "I really would like to go home."

"Just one more question. Please?" He gestured to the chair.

She sighed and sat down. Not even so much as a friendly grin from Graham Burke; he was all business.

"Now, Ms. Ridgeway—may I call you Tess?" Iverson asked. "Tess, we've run into a roadblock. Frankly, we can't find any reason why someone would want Tommy Vincenza dead. The picture we get is of a vulgar, harmless clown who was no threat to anybody. Is that the way you saw him?"

"Pretty much."

"Did you ever see him in the company of Joey LaCosta outside the Corner Bar?"

That's two questions. "I never saw either one of them outside the Corner Bar, together or separately."

"Hmm." Cheryl started inching over toward their table, wiping her hands on a towel; Iverson saw her coming but pretended he didn't. He said, "Do you know any reason at all why he might have been killed, Tess?"

Cheryl was by their table. Tess glanced up at her and said, "No, I don't."

"Yes, you do, Tess," Cheryl blurted out. "Tommy was blackmailing Phil!"

"Jesus Christ!" Phil yelled from behind the bar.

"You were there, Tess," Cheryl insisted. "You heard it too."

Graham was looking from one woman to the other. "Tess?"

Tess gritted her teeth and said, "I heard Tommy insisting that Phil couldn't fire him, and Phil never denied it. That's all." She turned to the waitress. "Cheryl, you don't really believe Phil killed Tommy."

"Of course not! But if Tommy was squeezing Phil, he coulda been squeezing somebody else as well, couldn't he?"

Iverson was leaning back in his chair, his hands folded comfortably over his well-padded middle and his protruding eyes half shut. He directed a big-toothed smile in the direction of the bar. "Mr. Maynard! Why don't you come join us?"

Phil muttered something under his breath and took his time getting there. Graham drew up chairs for Cheryl and Phil, making five people who were crowded around the small table. Phil sat there glowering at Cheryl. "You're fired."

She flapped a hand at him. "No, I'm not. Phil, don't you see? If we don't help them all we can, they're going to go on thinking the Corner Bar's part of LaCosta's scat operation. You don't want that, do you?"

"She has a point," Tess said mildly.

There was silence for a moment, until Iverson sat up abruptly and rubbed his hands together. "Well! Now that you've all decided to cooperate with the police, let's hear it. What did Tommy have on you, Mr. Maynard?"

"It has nothin' to do with what happened tonight."

"Let me be the judge of that, please. Well?" Phil didn't answer. "Mr. Maynard, do I have to point out that you are our only suspect?"

Graham leaned toward Phil. "Let's put it this way, Maynard. You tell us right now, or we're taking you downtown and booking you."

"Shit." Phil looked as if he wanted to punch someone. "All right. Tommy found out I paid off a building inspector. Bastard wouldn't let me open without a kickback."

Iverson made a tsk-tsking sound. "Corruption in city government, will it never end? We'll want the name of the inspector and the particulars. But how much was Tommy soaking you for?"

"I paid Tommy union minimum and not a penny more," Phil said hotly. "You can check the books!" Then some of the anger went out of him. "All Tommy ever wanted from me was a stage and a spotlight."

Iverson nodded. "But as long as you provided him with that stage and spotlight, he continued to attract a criminal element to your place of business, did he not?"

"*I didn't kill Tommy!* I didn't like his routine and I sure as hell didn't like seeing LaCosta in my place, but . . ." Phil held his hands up helplessly. "But that's just not reason enough to kill him."

Tess agreed, and Lt. Iverson looked as if he did too. Cheryl said, "I know you didn't kill him, Phil."

"Oh gee thanks, Cheryl. That means a lot."

At that moment, Joey LaCosta came charging in from Phil's office. He stopped by Lt. Iverson and said, "I'm leaving. I cooperated with you guys, but now I'm through cooperating. You got nothing on me, and I'm leaving. You want to talk to me again, see my lawyer." He walked out without waiting for an answer.

Stefanovich had followed him out. "I'm sorry, Lieutenant, I just couldn't hold him any longer."

Iverson waved a hand dismissively. "We have nothing to

charge him with anyway. Unless it turns out that he and Mr. Maynard here are in partnership."

"For Christ's sake, *I'm* not LaCosta's partner!" Phil snarled. "You gotta look in your own department for that!"

The heads of all three policemen snapped toward him. "What do you know about that?" Iverson barked.

"Only that LaCosta is partners with or is payin' off or has *some* connection with a cop."

"How do you know that?" Graham asked.

Phil turned his hands palms up. "Tommy liked to brag. He was puttin' the squeeze on the cop." He snorted. "And you say I'm your *only* suspect! Tommy was a threat to whatever deal LaCosta had made with the police. LaCosta musta sent one of his goons back to the dressing room to take care of it."

Graham shook his head. "Stefanovich and I kept our eyes on LaCosta all evening. No one left the table from the time we got here until Tess came running out with the word about Tommy."

"That's right, Lieutenant," Stefanovich said.

"Who's the cop?" Iverson demanded.

"No idea," Phil answered. "Tommy wasn't givin' away his meal ticket."

"It's all a bunch of horseshit anyway," Graham said in disgust. "Everyone loves to think *dirty cop.*"

"Well, well." Iverson scratched his balding head. "It seems our harmless comic wasn't so harmless after all."

They went over it again, and then again, Iverson urging Phil to remember Tommy's exact words. Tess stopped listening; she was so tired she was drooping.

Graham noticed. "Lieutenant, would it be all right if we let the women go home? It's late."

"Of course, how thoughtless of me," Iverson agreed immediately. "I thank you for your help, ladies. You go on home now."

"I'll walk you to your car," Graham said to Tess. Stefanovich picked up the cue and offered his services to Cheryl.

Outside, the air was damp as well as chilly. "Where are you parked?" Graham asked.

Tess had to think. "Down here. Left side of the street." They walked in silence for a moment or two. "You can't seriously suspect Phil," she said. "All he's guilty of is bribing a city official, and he was more or less forced into that."

Graham smiled sourly. "I wish I had a dollar for every time I've heard a felon confess to a lesser crime to divert suspicion from a larger one. Nope, Maynard's our best bet."

"Well, I think you're wrong. Here we are, my car's right over—oh, no! *Awww, no!*"

The car had been stripped. All four tires were gone. The trunk had been sprung and the spare taken as well. The hood was up; the thieves had helped themselves to the battery plus a few other parts. They'd taken her tape deck, radio, and her Jack Teagarden tapes. They'd even taken the boots and umbrella she kept in the back seat.

"Thieving sonsabitches," Graham muttered. "Let me call it in and then I'll drive you home."

He followed her inside when she unlocked the door. Hugo was nowhere in sight, she was glad to see; the last thing she needed tonight was a cat attack. By the time Tess had left for the Corner Bar earlier that evening, Hugo had fully recovered from the trauma of his visit to the vet and was back to his normal nasty self.

Tess dumped her gown, her raincoat, and her purse on a chair and collapsed onto the sofa. She was feeling numb;

the cannibalizing of her car had capped the day perfectly. It would be a day to remember, all right.

"Do you need a drink?" Graham asked her. "Or coffee? How about something to eat?"

She shook her head. "Shouldn't I be saying those things to you?"

"I don't want anything. But you're looking kind of down."

She laughed shortly. "Why should I feel down? Everything's peachy keen. I sing trash during the day for money so I can go into that crummy bar at night and sing a kind of music that had its heyday over sixty years ago. I live with a cat that hates me. I'm involved in a murder. And my car has just been stripped. Why should I feel down?"

He gave her a small smile. "Where do you keep the booze?"

"Kitchen."

He went into the kitchen and fixed her a drink. "You have a cat?" he said, handing her the glass. "I like cats. Where is she?"

"He. Around, someplace." She took a sip; scotch again, but not the smooth stuff Cheryl had brought her at the Corner Bar. Tess put the glass down; she didn't want the drink. She caught a glimpse of a small, gray, furry face peeking around the doorjamb; Hugo was watching Graham, checking out this intruder into his private space.

"Tess, I think you need to get to bed. I'm going to leave you my card, and I want you to call me if things get too bad. Will you do that?" Graham started feeling through his pockets. "I can never find my card case when I want it."

While he fumbled through his pockets, Tess watched Hugo ease around the doorjamb into the room. He hid behind a potted plant, his eyes still fixed on Graham. "Just write it down for me," she said.

"No, I got it here someplace. Oh, *hell*." He went over to a table and started emptying his pockets. A notebook, loose change, keys, two ballpoint pens, a pocket knife, a ring.

A ruby ring. Tommy's ruby ring, the one LaCosta gave him and he'd been so proud of.

Graham? *Graham Burke?* Tess turned her head away quickly.

But she hadn't been quick enough. Graham heaved a long, sad sigh. "That wasn't too smart of me, letting you see the ring," he said. "But it wasn't too smart of you, letting me know you'd seen it." He gathered up his belongings and put them back in his pocket. "Ah, Tess, Tess! I didn't want this to happen."

They stared at each other, the air electric between them. "You killed Tommy," she said in a high tight voice. "*You* are LaCosta's cop?"

A muscle in his face twitched; he didn't like her putting it that way. "We all have our own ways of surviving. Tommy was getting to be a problem. That was his way of surviving, you know—collecting for not talking. LaCosta's not what you'd call discreet. He gave just enough away that Tommy was able to put two and two together. I couldn't let it go on, Tess."

She pressed the flats of her hands against her temples. "You actually put that rope around his . . . why did *you* do it? That seems more like LaCosta's line of work!"

"LaCosta didn't know. If he'd found out a little prick like Tommy Vincenza could put the screws on me—well, it could queer our arrangement. And I'm not going to let *anything* queer our arrangement."

She understood. She took a breath and said, "What are you going to do?"

"I got to figure this out. I don't want to kill you, Tess."

"Then don't! Do you really think I'd say anything if I knew it would get me killed?"

"Keep quiet for a minute, will you?" He lowered himself onto an armchair opposite her, tense and stiff.

Tess jumped up and started pacing, trying desperately to think of a way out. Absently she noticed Hugo crawling on his stomach toward Graham; the damned cat was stalking him. *Atta boy, Hugo! Come charging to the rescue!* She was having trouble concentrating.

"You aren't going to try anything foolish, like running for the door?" He took his gun out of his shoulder holster and held it on the end table to his right.

"No." She stopped her pacing and picked up a pewter box that was said to have belonged to Billie Holiday; musical notes were engraved on the top. She opened and closed the lid nervously, the box's weight giving her something solid to hold on to. "Graham, let's try to work something out. I—I'll go out and commit a crime and you can take pictures and—"

"Don't be foolish!" he snapped.

"But there's got to be another way!" She opened and closed the lid of the box. *I am actually standing here thinking about attacking an armed man with a pewter box.* "I'm not Tommy Vincenza. I'm not going to make trouble for you." If she could just get to the phone . . .

He grunted, didn't answer. Hugo was crouched under the end table that Graham was resting his gun on.

Tess saw the exact moment he decided to kill her. The tension disappeared, replaced by a kind of euphoria. The deciding was the hard part, not the doing. A loose sort of smile appeared on his face, and he said, "I'm sorry, Tess. I really am."

She knew there was no point in trying to talk him out of it now. "You're a stupid man, aren't you?" she said sharply. "Solving your problems with violence—the first resort of the stupid man. A surefire sign of failure."

He just laughed, rather enjoying the situation now that he'd made up his mind she had to die. "Ah, Tess, I don't have to justify myself. All I have to do is figure out *how*. Why don't you put on some music? I like music while I'm thinking."

"Go to hell."

He didn't seem to hear her. "Perhaps an accident? Nope, Iverson would see right through that. I guess you'll have to go the same way Tommy did."

Maybe she could throw the box at him and run for the door. He was almost ignoring her; Tess the person had already ceased to exist for him. He just smiled that loose smile and stretched out his legs, crossing them at the ankles. He looked completely relaxed.

Hugo emerged from under the table and started sniffing at his feet. "Why, here's your cat! Hello, kitty." He switched his gun to his left hand and reached his right down toward Hugo. Hugo hissed. "What's the matter with him?"

"He's . . . shy." Tess swallowed. "He, ah, he loves to have his back stroked, though."

"Most cats do." He put his hand on Hugo's back.

Tess made her move. The minute Hugo sank his teeth into Graham's hand, she raised the pewter box in the air and brought it down as hard on the detective's head as she could, cutting off his yelp of pain and surprise. The gun fell to the floor, and Graham toppled forward on his face. Hugo bolted from the room.

Phone. Call for help. But Graham was moving, groaning and trying to get up on his hands and knees. Tess felt a flash of panic. This wasn't the way it happened on television—he was supposed to pass out long enough for her to call the police! She hit him again. He fell forward again, still groaning. She dropped the box and picked up his gun. She pointed it at him, wondering if she would have to shoot him.

No, this wouldn't do. *Call the police, call the police!* She put the gun on the table and started looking through Graham's clothing; she found the handcuffs tucked into his belt in the back. Tess jerked his arms around behind him and cuffed his wrists together. That done, she just sat down on the floor, *plop*. It took her a couple of minutes to stop trembling.

Then she made the call.

By the time the police took Graham Burke away, he was fully conscious, demanding medical attention and loudly denying his guilt. He even went so far as to accuse Tess of murdering Tommy and then planting the ring on him. The police seemed wholly unimpressed.

Lt. Iverson stayed behind. "Are you sure you're all right, Tess?"

"I'm fine." And she was, now that it was over. "I don't see how he did it. He was sitting there all evening, right next to his partner—what's his name, Stefanovich."

"I imagine Stefanovich will tell us that Burke left the table to go to the men's room at least once. Stefanovich was there to watch LaCosta, remember, not his partner."

"And you had no idea Graham Burke was connected?"

Iverson heaved a heavy sigh. "We were sure LaCosta had *some* cop in his pocket. That's why he's still walking around free. We could never catch him with the goods—he always seemed to know where and when we were going to show up with a search warrant. We'll get him now, though. But to

answer your question, nothing pointed to Burke in particular."

Tess nodded. "Why'd he take the ring? Simple theft?"

"No, he recognized it as LaCosta's. He was trying to divert attention away from his partner. That was his job, protecting LaCosta. Remember how quick he was to alibi him?
Burke was trying to throw suspicion on Phil Maynard."

"Where is Phil? Did you arrest him?"

"Oh, I sent him home hours ago," Iverson said. "The
man was clearly innocent."

For the first time in hours, Tess smiled. "Lieutenant, you
are a treasure."

"That's what I tell my wife every night." Iverson smiled
back, big-toothed and friendly. "Well, good night, Tess.
Lock up tight."

"I will." When he was gone, Tess stood in the middle of
the living room for a few minutes, doing nothing, thinking
nothing, enjoying the silence. It had been an ugly night.

Then she started a systematic hunt for the cat. She
found him in her bedroom closet, crouched down behind
the shoe rack. Tess sat on the floor outside the closet, trying
to make herself less menacing. "Hello, Hugo," she said
softly. "You don't even know you saved my life tonight, do
you?"

The cat stared at her, not moving.

"You certainly earned your right to live here, you know
. . . not that you need to. You *have* the right. But I thank you
just the same. Can I get you something? Sardines? Lobster?
A gallon of whipped cream?"

Hugo hissed.

Tess didn't mind. "That's all right, Hugo, you take your
time," she said. "I'll wait."

In spite of its title, this story is not about food and cooking—so, no recipe. Instead, the story tells of a bickering family that unexpectedly discovers one of its members is in danger. And by the way, do you know the French word for "asparagus"?

FRENCH ASPARAGUS

One reason I liked Julie was that she never got *that* tone in her voice whenever I was slow to understand. Mom would use the words of courtesy like "Please" and "Concentrate, dear"; but her tone was saying "Don't be such a dummy." My brother Noah was even better at it than Mom. He'd say "Speak more slowly so Sis can understand"—and then look around to make sure everyone saw how patient he was being. But everyone knew he was really calling me a nitwit.

I'm not a nitwit, but I was fourteen or fifteen before I figured that out. I just have no gift for languages, that's all. When Dad died, Mom quit her job as a Spanish teacher, took the insurance money, and started up a translation agency. Since Noah absorbed new languages through his pores, he joined Mom in the business as soon as he finished college. But when in spite of my best efforts, I could never get higher than a C in high school French, it was understood that I would have to find something else to do with my life. Okay by me.

The agency prospered; they hired more staff and moved

into larger quarters. Much of the revenue came from the translation of technical manuals, of which there seemed to be an abundance of new ones every month. But there Mom and Noah ran into a snag; neither of them knew Japanese. That's when they hired Julie, born in Tokyo, to American parents and a resident of Japan the first twelve years of her life.

So when Noah married Julie, I thought that meant a third person would be talking down to me. But Julie never did that. Her words and her voice always fit together right. But I've been wondering about Julie; maybe she's not as smart as she seems. I mean, if she was smart, why did she want to be married to Noah?

"*Donne-moi le beurre,*" Noah said to me.

I passed him the butter.

"Congratulations, Beth," he said with a smirk. "A red-letter day."

"Stop teasing your sister, Noah," Mom said as she cut her meat into teeny tiny pieces. "She does the best she can."

I bristled. "Poor little Beth, feel sorry for her?"

Mom sighed. "Beth, must you take exception to everything I say?"

"Sorry, Mom." And I was; it was Noah I was pissed at.

"The asparagus is delicious," Julie said brightly.

But Noah wasn't ready to quit. "Do you know what the French for asparagus is?"

I thought I did. "*Aubergine.*"

"That's 'eggplant'. For crying out loud, Beth, it's a simple cognate—*asperge*. You should know that." He turned his attention to his meal, having scored his point.

Dang, he made me mad. "And there speaks a man who can't even put a roll of film in a camera. Noah the Help-less."

"Well, really, Beth," Mom interrupted. "It's not as if your brother needs a camera to do his work."

I pounced. "Exactly. No more than I need to know the French for 'asparagus' to do mine."

"She has a point," Julie murmured.

"Julie, dear," Mom said through a clenched smile, "this is a family matter."

"And I'm not family?" replied Julie, her irritation showing.

Noah had put down his fork and was peering at me with fake curiosity. "You really consider that work? Taking pictures of corpses? You don't pose them or anything. You don't even have to worry about their fidgeting and spoiling the shot."

Oh, nice one. "Noah, what would you do without me to feel superior to?" I laughed. "Besides, you wouldn't last one day as a police photographer."

He shuddered. "I certainly hope not. But you wouldn't be so defensive about your job if you thought it was a real profession."

Julie said sharply, "She wouldn't need to defend herself if you'd just stop attacking for a while."

Noah threw up both hands. "Oh, great. Now even my wife has turned against me!"

Dysfunctional? You bet.

Mom insisted we all have dinner together once a week. Sometimes we ate out, but tonight she'd cooked. As a ploy to strengthen the family unit, it wasn't working too well. Noah and Julie had been fighting before they got there; they both put on a good front, but it still showed. I can maintain my civility with Noah *or* Mom, but the two of them together in the same room get to be a bit much. Mom tended to see herself as some sort of *grande dame* to whose wishes everyone catered. And when we didn't, she got cranky.

Right then she was telling us to stop bickering. "You are guests in my house," she reminded us, like Queen Victoria laying down the law, "and I expect you to behave accordingly. You should know better."

Julie stood up quickly. "Since my table manners aren't up to par, I'd better leave." And without another word, she walked out of the house. A moment later we heard the car start.

"Wonderful," Noah snarled. "Now how am I supposed to get home?"

"Taxi?" I suggested helpfully. "Feet?"

"Beth will give you a ride home," Mom declared flatly.

Noah looked horrified. "I'll call a taxi," he said hastily. I ride a motorcycle, which scares him to death. But Mom had decided that sister and brother should ride away together— a bonding experience, no doubt. So when it was time to go, Noah put on my extra helmet and manfully refrained from bursting into tears.

I didn't hit *every* bump on the way home.

The call came in the next afternoon at about three. Possible homicide, the Regent movie theater on Fremont. I gathered my gear together and climbed into the Crime Scene Unit van.

The Regent was showing something called *Invaders from Andromeda*. For once, the detectives had gotten to the site before we did—Ray Minelli and his new partner, some redheaded guy. The theater was empty except for a cleaning woman and a man I assumed was the manager. The Regent was a neighborhood theater and didn't show matinees during the week.

Minelli asked me to get the pictures fast before the medical examiner got there . . . but then held me up to make an introduction. "Beth, meet my new partner, Tony Brill. Tony, say hello to Beth Wasserman."

We both said hello. Brill had *rookie detective* written all over him and was champing at the bit. His first homicide? "It *is* homicide, isn't it?" I asked them.

"Stab wound in the back of the neck, no knife," Minelli said with a shrug.

"He was killed last night during the movie," Brill added. "He's slumped over sideways in his seat so the projectionist and the manager didn't notice him when they closed up. But he's been dead a while, all right. Rigor's well advanced."

"You touched him?"

Brill stared off into space. "Naw, I just looked."

Uh-huh. "I'd better get going."

In the auditorium, a couple of beat cops were protecting the crime scene. But when I saw the dead man slumped over sideways, my stomach did a flip. Whoever this poor guy was, he was the spitting image of my brother Noah. Same age, same approximate height and weight, same coloring. Even his facial features were similar.

Did you ever take pictures of a dead man who looks like your own brother? Well, I'll tell you, some really weird things pop into your head at a time like that. Like: *Did the hit man get the wrong guy?* And: *What had Noah and Julie been arguing about last night?* All the time I kept reeling off shots automatically, even carrying on a kind of conversation with the two cops.

But on the way back to develop the film, I came out of my mini-shock. What was the matter with me? Julie was the *nice* one in the family! The idea of her hiring a hit man was preposterous. Besides, well, it wasn't her place to kill Noah.

Noah's a snot, let's face it; but he's my brother and nobody has the right to kill him except *me*.

While the film was in the developer, I called Noah at the agency and asked if he'd seen a movie called *Invaders from Andromeda*.

"Yeah, I just saw it last night. Why?"

"Last night? I took you home last night."

He gave one of his be-patient-with-her sighs. "Julie wasn't home and I got fidgety so I went to a movie. What's the big deal?"

"No big deal. *Invaders from Andromeda*—er, that's at the Regent, isn't it? Is it any good?"

"The Regent, right. It's okay, kind of noisy. Since when have you started calling me for movie reviews?"

"Since today," I said, and hung up.

I made some extra prints of the dead man for myself. The victim's name turned out to be Jack Nimitz; he was a clerk in a shoe store who'd spent his evening watching stalwart earth warriors fight off intergalactic invaders. Nimitz had a clean sheet; he was single, shy, lived in a one-bedroom apartment in the Arlington section of town. No enemies, not in trouble of any kind. Harmless.

Minelli and Brill were doing their usual thing of investigating the victim to find his killer. But when by noon the next day they'd uncovered not even a hint of a reason why anyone would want him dead, I began wondering again about his eerie resemblance to Noah.

I called Julie and asked her to meet me for lunch.

We met at the Café d'Antibes where I'd reserved a booth so we could talk privately. Julie didn't look so hot; she had circles under her eyes and her mouth was drawn into a straight line. *Something* was bothering her.

I waited until she'd had time to eat most of her lunch before I started. "Julie, the night before last, when you walked out of Mom's house—where did you go?"

She looked pained. "That was a dumb thing to do. I apologized to Mom."

"Never mind that. Where did you go?"

Julie shot me a questioning look but said, "Oh, I didn't want to go home and wait for Noah. He'd be mad when he got there and I just wasn't ready to deal with that. So I drove around for a bit and ended up at the Amusement Pier. Bright lights and happy faces, that's what I needed."

"Did you see anyone you knew?"

"No, I . . ." Her voice trailed off and her eyes grew wide. "That sounds as if you're asking for an alibi. Beth, what's this all about?"

I took out my envelope of 8 x 10 glossies. "I had to shoot a homicide scene yesterday. I want you to take a look at the victim."

She wasn't too happy with that. "You want me to look at pictures of a corpse?"

"It's important, Julie." I slid the photographs from the envelope and spread them out on the table.

She gasped. "My god! He could be Noah's twin! Who is he?"

"His name's Jack Nimitz. He was a shoe store clerk, lived a quiet life. The detectives on the case can't find any reason anyone might want him dead. Julie, do you know where Noah went? The night you ended up at the Amusement Pier?"

The seeming change of subject threw her for a moment, but she said, "I think he went to a movie. Why?"

"Look at the pictures again. This time, look at the surroundings."

She did. "A movie theater!"

I nodded. "The same movie theater where Noah went. The same night."

She looked horrified. "Are you saying *Noah* killed him?"

"No, no!" What an idea. "But try to visualize it. A darkened movie theater. Two men who look alike. Couldn't the killer simply have made a mistake?"

She seemed to shrink when she understood what I was getting at. "Oh, my god. Someone is trying to kill Noah?" She wriggled out of the booth. "Come on! We've got to warn him!"

"It's just a theory, Julie."

"I know that. But we can't take the chance."

I got her to wait long enough for us to pay the bill, and then we ran most of the three blocks to the agency's building. Mom's translating biz was on the eleventh floor, and the elevator had never seemed slower.

The door to my brother's office said **Noah Wasserman, Vice-President**. He looked up from his computer, irritated at the interruption, until Julie had explained and I'd showed him the photographs. Then the first thing he did was get up and lock the door.

Typically, he turned on me. "Why didn't you tell me right away? He had to have followed me from home to the theater, and he could be following me now! Why didn't you tell me?"

"Because I didn't know until today that Jack Nimitz was such an unlikely target. The detectives need *some* time to investigate, for Pete's sake. I don't even know whether *you* are a likely target or not. How about it, Noah? Is someone out to get you? Some serious enemy you've made that we don't know about?"

"No, of course not—don't be ridiculous," he said loudly.

Boy, did I know that look on his face. And I knew that

strangled voice. I even knew that strange fluttering of the fingers of his right hand that he did every time he was—

"You're lying," I said flatly. "Come on, Noah, you know I can tell when you're lying. What's going on?"

He looked miserable, something I would normally have enjoyed a great deal. "Mom said to keep my mouth shut."

"Mom?" I looked at Julie; she raised her hands, palms up. as much in the dark as I was. "Look. I've got to get back to work. Noah, I think you should ask for police protection—"

"I think so too, but I don't know if—Beth, you haven't told them, have you? About that guy's resemblance to me?"

"Not yet."

"Hold off a bit, will you?"

"All right, but there's something you two haven't thought of. If you were the intended victim, who's the first person the police are going to look at as a possible suspect?"

"I don't know," Noah said. "Who?"

"She means me," Julie said tiredly. "Yes, I've thought of that. But if Noah really is in danger . . ."

"All right. Truth, now. What were you two fighting about the other night?"

"Nothing," said Noah.

"Everything," said Julie.

That was a big help. "We're going to have to powwow tonight. Mom's house, eight o'clock. And I have got to get back to work."

I left them there together. On my way out I stopped by Mom's office and told her we'd all be descending upon her at eight that evening.

I had only one call that afternoon, a head-on collision on Belmont. Messy, but no one seriously hurt. The two drivers were moaning about their insurance companies when I left.

After I'd finished with that, I moseyed into the squad-room looking for Minelli or Brill. They were both there, both on the phone. I sat down by Minelli's desk and waited. He finished talking and hung up.

I asked, "Anything new on Jack Nimitz?"

"Naw, the guy was a nobody," Minelli said with a sigh. "No one had any strong feelings about him one way or the other. He was either the victim of a random act of violence or the killer whacked the wrong guy."

"The wrong guy?" I said, all innocence. "I suppose that could happen. It would have been dark in there—easy to make a mistake."

"Brill thinks we have a psycho on the loose." He nodded toward his partner's desk. "But it don't look like that to me. Too deliberate. One thrust of the knife in exactly the right place—kapooey! He's gone."

"So how do you go about looking for a killer who whacked the wrong guy?"

"Beats the hell out of me," he said.

I wanted to tell him right then. But first I needed to find out what Mom had to do with all this.

"We're being sued," Mom said.

Julie's eyebrows shot up. "Sued? The agency, you mean?"

"For ten million dollars," Noah said bitterly.

"Which is foolish," Mom added calmly. "We don't have ten million dollars. We can't *get* ten million dollars. It's a malicious suit brought for the sole purpose of putting us out of business."

Mom had recovered from the shock of the dead man's resemblance to Noah faster than any of the rest of us. She'd announced that the murder in the Regent movie house changed everything, and of course Noah must be protected at all costs. Then she told us the bad news.

Or part of it. "How about a few details here?" I asked. "Who's suing, and why?"

An uncomfortable silence developed. Finally Noah said, "Oh, some Kraut didn't like the way I translated one of his technical manuals."

"It's rather more serious than that, dear," Mom said reprovingly.

Little by embarrassing little, the story came out. The manual was distributed to new American customers for a whizbang new computer operating system the German company had been selling in Europe with great success. But the translation was so full of errors that even the American technical support people couldn't get the thing to work. The returns, the loss in sales and reputation—the fiasco had put a serious dent in the German company's business. And now the Germans were—quite rightly, I thought—suing the translation agency that was the cause of all their troubles.

"Beth, stop that!" Mom said sharply. "Get up!"

I'd laughed myself right off my chair. My snooty, condescending, know-it-all brother had screwed up so royally that Mom was in danger of losing her agency. *That* part wasn't funny, but all I could think of right then was that I'd never have to take any more lip from Noah for not knowing the French for asparagus.

I wiped my eyes and pulled myself up off the floor. When I saw the way Noah was glaring at me, I started laughing all over again. Mom was disgusted.

"German isn't my first language," Noah muttered in Mom's direction. "I told you to let me stick to French."

"Right, it's all Mom's fault," I said.

"Noah, dear, you know we were on a tight deadline,"

Mom said with an edge in her voice. "Sometimes we just have to pitch in where we're needed."

Julie spoke up. "I must be dense, but I don't see the connection. This German company wants to kill Noah?"

"Not the company, no," Mom said. "But they fired their main representative here for not, ah, checking more closely on the agency he hired to do the translating. He was very bitter. He came to the office and actually threatened us."

"He threatened you?" I asked. "With violence?"

"Yeah, the guy was really nuts," Noah muttered. "Went on and on about how he'd sold all his property in Germany because he thought he'd be living out the rest of his life in this country, stuff like that. Then suddenly he's out of a job and he blamed me for that."

Wonder why. "How did he threaten you? What did he say?"

"Oh, bunch of stuff, I don't know. He was so angry he could barely speak. I didn't even know who he was when he came in and started raving like that."

"So he met you in person only once, and that was at a time he was out of his head with anger?" I asked. "Then he *could* have mistaken Jack Nimitz for you in the theater."

"I'm sure that's what happened, dear," Mom said. "He struck me as a very dangerous man."

I sighed. "Would either of you care to tell me the name of this killer the police are even now out looking for?"

His name was Walter Buchholz, and no, dear, we don't know where he lives; why should we? I got Mom to write down his name and the address of the office the German company maintained here. Then I looked at Julie.

"You really didn't know about this, did you? That's not what you and Noah were fighting about at all."

She shook her head. "Noah and I—well, we just haven't

been getting along lately. We have an appointment with a marriage counselor next week."

Mom looked shocked. "You're going to tell intimate details of your private life to a stranger?"

Noah tried to bluster. "I'm not crazy about the idea, but Julie insisted. And if it makes her happy, hey, I'll go along." Big magnanimous Noah.

Julie was looking at him. "No wonder you've been impossible to live with lately. You should have told me, Noah."

"Yeah, well."

"I asked him not to, dear," Mom said sweetly.

"You should have told me," Julie repeated, ignoring Mom.

Noah was really wriggling, caught between the two of them. "Sort it out among yourselves," I told them. "I'm off."

"Where are you going?" Mom wanted to know.

"To find a detective named Minelli," I said.

Walter Buchholz was living at the same place he'd been living while he was still working for the German company that had sent him here; it was an easy matter for Minelli and Brill to find him. Minelli told me later at the stationhouse that they'd found him sitting in the dark, staring at nothing. The detective said it was as if he was paralyzed, once he found out he'd killed an innocent man and his nemesis was still walking around whole and hearty. Brill found the knife in a leather case in Buchholz's bureau, and the lab was able to bring up minute traces of Jack Nimitz's blood.

Then to sew it up, both the ticket-seller and the kid behind the refreshment counter at the Regent identified Buchholz as being in the theater two nights earlier, the night the killing took place. "Means, motive, and opportunity,"

Minelli chortled. "I'd hate to tell you how long it's been since I nailed a perp with all three. This guy's a textbook case."

"He's gonna confess," Brill said. "Just you watch."

Minelli grunted. "The guy's practically a zombie. He'll probably say whatever we want him to say."

And so Walter Buchholz was tried and convicted, a stranger who'd killed an inoffensive shoe salesman because he looked like my brother. I never spoke to Walter Buchholz; I never even saw him except at the trial. He was just some dangerous storm who blew through our lives and then was gone.

The agency still had the lawsuit hanging over it. The German company disavowed all responsibility for Buchholz's act, of course. But they sent word through their lawyers that they were now willing to negotiate.

The whole affair had a sobering effect on Noah. He was still a horse's patoot, but he'd lost a lot of his condescending attitude. We met for lunch at a vegetarian restaurant that had just opened; Noah fiddled with his menu and said, "I'm thinking about leaving the agency. Striking out on my own. A man can't go on working for his mother all his life."

Out of habit I almost called him on it—but stopped myself. I knew the Germans had offered to sue for only their loss of revenue . . . *if* Mom got rid of Noah. He was trying to salvage some self-respect out of the mess. "That sounds like a good idea, Noah. What does Julie think?"

"Oh, she's all for it," he said. "In fact, she sounded kind of relieved."

I'll bet she did. "Well, good luck, Bro." He looked at me suspiciously. "I mean it, Noah. Good luck."

And then I saw something on Noah's face I hadn't seen since I was five years old: a shy smile. I guess he wasn't any more used to hearing kind words from me than I was to hearing them from him.

Still grinning, he opened the menu and studied it. "All these veggies. What do you have a taste for?"

"*Aubergine,*" I said. "I'm getting kind of tired of asparagus."

Here is my first attempt at writing crime fiction, although not my first published story (that was science fiction). "The Favor" is not a mystery story in the traditional sense; it doesn't follow the standard pattern of crime → investigation → solution. A murder does take place, but it's not of primary concern. Rather it's the result of the murder that's the focus of the story—how it causes two men, virtual strangers to each other, to form a strange sort of bond that lasts over forty years.

THE FAVOR

The name of Roy Burkhart jumped out of the newspaper and slapped him across the eyes.

Cancer. Survived by. Hours of viewing.

Roy Burkhart. Dead.

Eddie Caputo lowered the newspaper and stared at nothing for a minute or so. Strange sensation, another minute to recognize what it was: he wanted to cry.

I wouldn't have known him if I bumped into him.

Eddie looked at the picture again. Forty years made a hell of a difference. Forty-three. The last time Eddie had seen Burkhart (forty-three years ago), the face had been thin and frightened. This face was moon-shaped. Cortisone, probably.

He folded the paper and placed it on the park bench beside him, one meaty hand holding it down so it wouldn't fly away. A college-age couple ambled by, playing huggy-bear and kissy-face. Eddie: oblivious to their passage.

Fifteen minutes were lost before Eddie's memories would allow him to return to the present. He stood up and began the long walk home.

Short walk, *short* walk! When he was still living on Larimer Avenue, he could walk ten times the distance without so much as a muscle twitch in the legs. But he was young then.

Eddie Caputo was no longer young. This bothered him only physiologically—creaking bones, shortness of breath. Philosophically, he never gave it a thought. Since he had never felt young, the passing of youth—Youth as world-view—meant little to him. He'd never had much chance to be a child.

His full name was Edward Giuseppe Caputo, the "Giuseppe" in honor of a not-quite-remembered grandfather who had abandoned a hopeless Naples to build a life for himself in the land of the free and the home of et cetera. Giuseppe had followed an older brother to the East Liberty section of Pittsburgh, where he had grown, worked, married, begat, aged. A shadow in a rocking chair to the grandchildren.

Eddie grew up on Larimer Avenue (pronounced *Larr-*mur), that breeding ground of Mafiosi back when being connected could mean the difference between surviving and not. It was a normal maturing period, normal for that place and that time, in which disagreements were settled by force or by a sufficient display thereof. Caught between the mob on one side and street gangs on the other, Eddie had talked his father into letting him attend North Side Trade School instead of regular high school. There he learned carpentry, wiring, plumbing, some iron work, brick-laying. A cement-finishing school.

North Side Trade School was located eight miles from Eddie's home on Larimer. He walked it twice a day, five days a week. A bitter walk in winter, but inescapable: the bus fare was fifteen cents each way. Thirty cents a day, a dollar and a half a week, six dollars a month. Impossible: the year was 1930.

To reach North Side Trade, Eddie had to cross the Allegheny River. Even then Pittsburgh had more bridges than any other city in the world; out of that vast selection, Eddie chose the Seventh Avenue Bridge to make his crossing. It was on the Seventh Avenue Bridge that he first saw Roy Burkhart.

The pedestrian walkway was narrow; it was difficult to pass someone going in the opposite direction without engaging in eye contact. The first time Eddie had passed the thin young man five or six years his senior, they had glanced at each other self-consciously. By the fourth or fifth meeting, they were nodding familiarly, as if each knew who the other was.

Within a few weeks they were saying *Hello, Morning, Howyuh*. They never stopped to talk, each bent earnestly upon crossing some threshold before a naughty-naughty bell rang. They did not exchange names or destinations, but the thin stranger always carried in one hand a loose-leaf notebook with an insignia on the cover: Western Pennsylvania Seminary. Eddie carried both his hands in his pockets.

Throughout the winter their little morning ritual continued. The two never passed each other going back in the opposite directions; West Penn Sem and North Side Trade observed different closing hours. Eddie looked forward to their daily encounters; the appearance of the thin young man never varied more than a minute or two from 8:15 and was a sign that Eddie's long trek was almost over.

Winter took more time in passing than it should, in Eddie's opinion. It wasn't until late April that the darkness lifted and grim outdoor faces began to relax. And on the first Friday in May, for the very first time, the stranger failed to appear on the Seventh Avenue Bridge.

Surprised, Eddie wondered if the fine spring day had made him dawdle. He took out Grandfather Giuseppe's watch: it said 8:16. Oh, well. Maybe today was a religious holiday or something.

Eddie thought no more about it until Monday when the stranger again failed to appear. Nor was he there Tuesday or Wednesday. Had he finished his studies? Was he sick? By Thursday Eddie was definitely worried, and Friday he left school early and headed straight for Western Pennsylvania Seminary.

"I want to see the dean," he said to a woman behind a desk.

"Which dean?"

"*The* dean."

After a moment's hesitation she ushered him into the office of someone who certainly looked like a dean. Eddie got straight to the point. "I'm worried about one of your students." He described the stranger the best he could. When Eddie mentioned the last time he saw him had been on May fourth, he could see a change come over the dean's face.

"I think you're talking about Roy Burkhart," he said.

"Well? Where is he? Is he all right?"

The dean paused. "Burkhart is in jail. He's been charged with murder."

Murder. In early childhood Eddie had learned that sometimes people kill other people, and sometimes those people were his neighbors. But that was Larimer Avenue; that had nothing to do with the stranger on the bridge.

The victim, the dean said, had been Burkhart's girl-friend. She was found stabbed to death in her bedroom on May the fourth. The police had come into the seminary and arrested Burkhart on the same day. Eddie sat stunned, trying to get used to the idea of his stranger as a murderer.

The dean watched him sympathetically. "It's a shock, isn't it? I find it hard to believe myself."

When Eddie could talk again, he asked, "When did the girl die?"

"That morning, early. The coroner fixed the time of death between eight and eight-thirty."

"Did she live in North Side?"

"Burkhart did, but his girl lived in Mount Lebanon."

Eddie felt his skin begin to tingle. Mount Lebanon was a section of Pittsburgh located to the south, a good twenty-five- or thirty-minute bus ride from the bridge. "And this happened on the morning of the fourth?"

"That's right."

"Then he couldn't have done it. On the fourth at 8:15 he was in the middle of the Seventh Avenue Bridge."

The dean's body jerked upright. *"What?"*

"He was on the bridge. Like every morning."

"Are you certain?"

"If we're talking about the same fella, I am. He was on the bridge."

The dean's hand shot out for the phone.

Eddie told his story to the police, then to some men from the District Attorney's office. He picked Burkhart out of a line-up. Yes, that's the guy. Yes, he was on the Seventh Avenue Bridge at 8:15, you could set your watch by him. On May fourth, that's a Thursday. Yes. Eddie repeated his story before a judge. He signed papers.

The charges against Roy Burkhart were dropped.

In a City-County Building hallway smelling of cleaning compound, the two young men faced each other. Burkhart had the look of a man who'd just been pulled out of a caved-in mine—stunned, not quite believing. "You know what they were going to do to me?" he said to Eddie. "They were going to put me in that chair in Harrisburg and pull the switch, if you hadn't come forward. They were really going to do that."

Eddie cleared his throat, didn't say anything.

"I told them about you, you know," Burkhart went on. "I told them I passed you every morning, but they didn't believe anything I said. Not *anything*. I didn't know your name or how to get in touch with you. They wouldn't even send a man out to walk the bridge, they were so sure I'd killed her."

"Yeah, I know," Eddie said. "Once they've fingered a guy, that's it."

"It doesn't seem possible," Burkhart murmured more to himself than to Eddie. "I still haven't figured out how this could have happened." He mused a moment and then roused himself. "You know and I know there's no way I can ever thank you adequately, Eddie Caputo. I'll never forget *that* name. If you'd been another kind of person, someone who couldn't be bothered finding out what happened to me, I'd be dead before the year was over."

Eddie shrugged, embarrassed. "I just got worried, that's all."

Burkhart smiled sadly. "That still makes you pretty rare. It's my good luck you're the worrying kind. And it's also luck that we both used the same bridge. If I'd crossed the Ninth Avenue Bridge instead of the Seventh, I'd still be inside. Justice shouldn't have to depend on luck."

"What are you going to do now? Are you going back to the seminary?"

Burkhart looked down at his shoes. "No. All that seems irrelevant now. In a way I don't understand. I don't know what I'm going to do yet."

They stood silent a moment. "Well," said Eddie, "whatever you decide, good luck."

"And to you, Eddie Caputo."

They shook hands and parted. It was the first and last conversation the two ever had.

Sixty-three-year-old Eddie Caputo had to stop to rest; the walk home from the park grew longer every time he made it. He sat on the stone steps of Peabody High School, deserted this late in the afternoon. It was the high school he had left to attend North Side Trade. Peabody High, alma mater of Kenneth Burke, Malcolm Cowley, and Gene Kelly. Eddie knew who Gene Kelly was.

The stone was cold, and Eddie felt his right buttock begin to turn numb. He waited only until he was breathing regularly again and then moved on.

Graduation, unemployment, desperation. The natural order of things.

Eddie's recently acquired skills in carpentry and the like were useless. Not exactly a boom year for building, 1931. Almost a year dragged by before Eddie found a steady job as busboy in The Sportsman's Club.

Inside the Club there appeared no sign of depression, economic or otherwise; the affluent had a way of remaining affluent. Eddie cleared away the dirty dishes left by steel mill owners, prostitution-ring operators, lawyers, city council members, heroin distributors. The tips were generous and

Eddie was surprised to find he was earning a decent living. He listened to his mother and got married.

Two weeks after the wedding, one of the Club's customers handed Eddie a fifty-dollar bill, told him the name of a horse and an address. Eddie placed the bet and was given two dollars for his trouble. Soon he was running that same errand for all the pony-players in the Club. When his wife became pregnant, he started taking bets himself.

By the time his first son was born, Eddie had left his busboy job and was living on what he made as a bookie. And living well; he was taking in more money than he'd ever believed possible. He couldn't bank it, of course; the take was stored in a shoe box in the attic.

The only sour note was sounded by his wife, an ultra-religious woman who claimed that the money was tainted and that Eddie was well on his way to hell. She begged him, literally begged him on her knees in a melodramatic posture that embarrassed Eddie terribly, to give up taking bets and get an honest job. As a waiter. Or a brick-layer.

But Eddie didn't want to be a brick-layer. He liked what he did and he liked the kind of life it let him lead; no more walking sixteen miles a day because he didn't have the thirty cents bus fare. What he had then suited him: good money, a lot of movement, no nine-to-five. He never bet the horses himself; no successful bookie ever did. The percentage lay with betting against the bettors, not the horses.

One night a priest had rung Eddie's doorbell and handed him a familiar-looking shoe box. The priest had said wryly that while the Church appreciated Mrs. Caputo's donation, twenty-three thousand dollars was perhaps more than her husband would wish her to give away. After that, the money stayed in the shoebox, but Eddie was careful never to let his wife know where it was.

She prayed for him.

By 1941 Eddie had three sons and five shoe boxes. The Caputos were living in a house Eddie had built himself with the help of an uncle who worked as a foreman for a construction firm. They were comfortable and content, except for his wife's periodic outbursts about tainted money. The three boys always watched these displays with interest and somehow managed never to take sides. Smart kids. Eddie approved.

Early in June an envelope with no return address appeared in the mail. Eddie opened it to find a letter—no, it was one of those new xerographs, a picture made of a letter without a negative intermediary. And it wasn't a letter, it was an interoffice memo. The office was that of the District Attorney, and the memo was addressed to Roy Burkhart.

The whole incident of the bridge sprang to life in Eddie's memory where it had lain dormant for ten years. So Burkhart had gone into law enforcement. And was working for the D.A. Funny the effect certain experiences had on different people; if it had been Eddie who'd been wrongly accused, he wouldn't have wanted to work for the law after that.

The writer of the memo referred Mr. Burkhart to the included list of names and addresses of known bookmakers and numbers writers. The memo outlined a plan for simultaneous raids on said addresses. Date and hour to be transmitted verbally, as agreed.

The third name on the list was Edward G. Caputo.

Eddie burned the memo and all his betting slips. He collected his five shoe boxes, placed them in a suitcase, and checked the suitcase at the bus station. Then he phoned his construction foreman uncle.

When the men from the D.A.'s office burst into Eddie's

home, Eddie was patching potholes on Route 30.

He stayed with the job another year and then talked his uncle into quitting and going into business with him. The uncle's know-how and Eddie's shoe boxes made it work; in six or seven years they had a business that returned a reasonable, steady profit.

Eddie's wife now said prayers of thanksgiving. Now they lived on honest money, earned from honest labor. She never tired of telling Eddie how happy she was he had gone into honest work. Eddie never said anything to change her opinion of the construction industry.

As Eddie hauled his wheezing body up the front steps to his house, a *yip-yip-yip* greeted him from inside. He unlocked the door and bent over to fondle the quivering little dog-body that had been his sole companion in the big house for the past two years. Eddie's wife was dead, the boys married and with families of their own.

Off with the coat. Into the kitchen. Open the can. The little dog nipped gently at his ankles to hurry him along.

Eddie left the dog to his supper and climbed the stairs to the second floor. At the top he thought once again about turning one of the downstairs rooms into a bedroom.

In his room, he opened the closet and took out a dark suit, wondering if there would be time to have it cleaned before the funeral.

"Portrait" was written for an anthology of historical mystery short stories, and for this one I returned to a setting I'd used before, in a novel trilogy—A Cadenza for Caruso, Prima Donna at Large, *and* A Chorus of Detectives. *The time is 1918, the place is the Metropolitan Opera House, and the production is* La Bohème. *Geraldine Farrar returns to a role she hasn't sung in years, aided (or hampered) by her two favorite co-stars, Enrico Caruso and Antonio Scotti. I owe the title to M. D. Lake, who claims he didn't have the nerve to use it himself. I held on to it for over a year, until just the right story came along.*

Incidentally, this story gave one of my cats her name. She'd only recently moved in and stuck close to me the whole time I was writing, demanding constant attention. I got to the part of the story where the tenor sings "Mimi! Mimi!" at the end of La Bohème— *so of course I sang it. And suddenly there's this little cat sitting on my keyboard saying "Pirrup?" Which is cat language for "You called?"*

PORTRAIT OF THE ARTIST
AS A YOUNG CORPSE

I love young singers, really I do. They bring their innocent young faces and pure young voices to an old art form and infuse it with energy and vitality and the kind of hope possible only in the very young. I love the way the young women gamely sing supporting roles and openly lust after my star status—they're so sweet. "Oh, Miss Farrar," they simper, "you're the reason I decided to become an opera singer!" Some of them probably even mean it.

And the young men are even sweeter; they have this tendency to *worship,* you know, and not always from afar, bless their ambitious little hearts. One of them, a blue-eyed Viking from Minnesota, had told me six times how honored he was to be singing on the same stage as The Great Geraldine Farrar. His capitals, but I didn't argue the point.

Every year, a few promising newcomers; but in November of 1917 we had a whole crop of them. Gatti-Casazza, still managing the Metropolitan Opera in his own unique way, had announced to a roll of drums and a fanfare of trumpets that the Met would hereafter seek out American-trained singers—thus making himself appear wonderfully patriotic as well as admirably sensitive to the wishes of his adopted homeland. Because of the war, all the German singers were gone, and all German works had been banned from the *repertoire.* That left quite a few gaps to be filled.

So we began the 1917–1918 season with the house crowded with new artists—most of them in their early twenties, all of them eager to be liked, and every single one of them scheming like the very devil to edge one another out. They were soloists, not choristers, and they were being given the chance to show their stuff, mostly in small roles . . . and then work their way up to bigger ones if they were good enough. A chance to learn and gain experience at the same time.

As for me, I never went through that sort of apprenticeship. I started out at the top . . . and stayed there. I was nineteen years old when I first stepped out on the stage of the Royal Opera House in Berlin and sang Marguérite in

Faust. That was sixteen years ago, and I've been singing leads ever since.

"*Cara mia,*" Scotti murmured in my ear, "that young man is in love with you."

"Oh? Which young man is that?" I honestly didn't know, for once.

"The sad little puppy dog cowering in the corner."

Oh yes . . . *that* one. I knew his name. "Willis? Wallace? The baritone."

"The baritone who wants *my* roles," Scotti proclaimed in mock outrage.

They all wanted our roles, grasping little creatures that they are. I could barely see Willis-Wallace because of the crowd; he looked kind of pitiful, hanging around the edges of the group of well-wishers who'd come backstage. Scotti and I had just finished performing *Tosca*, the second production of the new season. (I could have strangled Gatti-Casazza when he decided to open the season with *Aïda*; I don't sing Verdi.) We were surrounded by friends; I would like to have spoken to Willis-Wallace, but talking was difficult. So I caught his eye and smiled and waved.

The change that came over that young baritone was nothing short of miraculous. His eyes widened, his face lit up, he broke into a smile. He straightened up and held his head high . . . good heavens, he was a foot taller than I'd realized.

"Gerry?" Scotti said peevishly. "If you finish with your flirting, we leave now?"

I laughed and took his arm. Antonio Scotti is miserable when he is not in love, and most of the time he's in love with me. Now was one of those times, again, and that suited me fine; we'd both just emerged from love affairs gone sour. Mine was worse than his—I'd actually married my lover.

Scotti would propose again before the week was out, and I'd say no again. I adore the man, but I'd be a fool to marry someone who falls in love as easily—and as often—as Scotti does.

But before we could reach the stagedoor, one of the other young artists in the company elbowed his way through the crowd to us. It was the blue-eyed Viking from Minnesota, with a tenor voice as robust as his physique. He was outgoing and rather pleased with himself, the exact opposite of Willis-Wallace who cowered in a corner waiting for a smile to be tossed his way.

The Viking's name was Albert Somethingson. "Oh, Miss Farrar!" he crooned. "You were *exquisite* tonight! Your *Vissi d'Arte* brought tears to my eyes. Never have I been so moved!"

The boy would go far. "Why, thank you, Albert. How charming of you to say so."

"When you ended your sigh with that little gasp, I had to clamp my hands over my mouth to keep from crying out!"

"And that," said Scotti, "is good place for them, I think. *Cara mia?* We go now?"

Albert burst out, "Miss Farrar? Would you do me the honor of having a late supper with me?"

But Scotti had had enough of all this adulation, especially since none of it was directed at him. "The lady," he announced in crushing tones, "is with *me*." He hurried me toward the stagedoor exit.

"Perhaps lunch tomorrow?" Albert called after us. "Or tea?" More desperately: "May I bring you breakfast?"

I just fluttered a gloved hand at him as we left; such invitations must never be answered with an unequivocal *no*.

The day after a performance is a day for resting the

voice. I did nothing more strenuous than a few mild vocal exercises to keep the physical equipment limber and spent most of the morning answering correspondence. A costume-fitting was scheduled for that afternoon; but as soon as the dressmaker left, I had a visitor.

Gatti-Casazza's usual way of communicating was by telephone or written notes; the fact that the general manager had come himself instead of sending a minion meant he wanted something from me. I was immediately on my guard.

He looked worried. "It is Frances," he said in lugubrious tones. "She undergoes emergency appendectomy this morning."

"How unpleasant for her," I replied. "Is she all right?"

"Yes, yes . . . there are no complications. I will give her your good wishes."

I hadn't offered any. Frances Alda was a soprano-not-so-extraordinaire who gave herself airs, carrying on as if she were an Olive Fremstad or a Lillian Nordica. Alda was a second-rate singer at best, but she assured her place at the Metropolitan when she married Gatti-Casazza. Everyone who'd ignored her before suddenly became sweet as pie to the general manager's wife.

Everyone except me.

"If she is in no danger," I said, "then what worries you so?"

"The recovery period," he replied. "She will not be able to sing Mimi on the sixteenth."

Ah, *that* was what he wanted! "Gatti, you know I haven't sung Mimi for six or seven years."

He went on about how this soprano was out of town and that soprano was singing the night before and so on. He could fill the role with a house soprano, but he wanted a star. "Think of it, Gerry—you and Caruso and Scotti, on stage together again. It will be standing room only!"

So Caruso was the bait. Gatti had not scheduled the two of us to sing together this season, not even once. Caruso always packed the house and I always packed the house; Gatti could sell more tickets when we sang separately. But I no longer considered *La Bohème* part of my *repertoire* and said so.

He turned on the charm, or tried to. "Ah, but Gerry—I know that *eccellente* memory of yours. A few days with a coach, a little study, it comes back, no? I schedule special rehearsal, just for you."

The truth was, I wouldn't mind performing the role again. And even on a bad day I could sing a better Mimi than Alda ever could. "I'd require more than my usual fee."

He sighed heavily. "Already I am overbudgeted."

"But only in the books you keep to show the artists. In the *real* books, there is money."

We fell into our usual haggling pattern and eventually settled on a figure. I shooed Gatti out; there was much to do if I was to sing Puccini's frail young seamstress in less than a week's time.

"Rico, you must promise me one thing," I said sternly to Caruso. "No practical jokes. No flour in the men's hats, no mousetraps on my skirts. I haven't sung Mimi in a long time, and I need your help instead of your hindrance."

"*Per dio!* You think I make the trouble for you?" His big black eyes opened wide, all innocence. "Never, Gerry! I help."

"I hope you mean that."

He looked hurt. "Do I lie to you? Ever?"

"Constantly."

"But I never mean it!"

"Rico. Behave yourself?"

"I behave, I behave!"

The special rehearsal Gatti-Casazza had arranged was being held in a rehearsal hall upstairs instead of on the stage. The orchestra had been reduced to one lone pianist, and the chorus consisted of eight singers instead of its full contingent of one hundred sixty. Caruso and I had just finished the duet that closes Act I, and I was pleased with the way things were going. I'd sung half-voice, in the German style of rehearsing. The Italians all sang full voice; they can't help it.

When I'd first sung *Bohème* with Caruso, in Monte Carlo, he'd picked me up and carried me off the stage at the end of Act I. But we were both older now, and one of us was a lot heavier and I don't mean me.

Both my young admirers were in the cast. Willis-Wallace was singing Schaunard, one of the four Bohemians who shared the attic that was the setting of the first and last acts. It was a utility role; he had no aria. Albert was singing the toy vendor, Parpignol; he had one flashy and joyful appearance in Act II and then dropped out of the opera. It was a lesser role than Schaunard.

Willis-Wallace was hovering again, not daring to approach; I always found shyness becoming in a young man—when it wasn't carried too far. So when Caruso had to answer a call of nature, I motioned to the young baritone to join me. At first he couldn't believe I meant him, and then he tripped over his own feet in his haste to reach my chair.

"The rehearsal is going well, don't you think?" I asked.

"You were *magnificent,*" he gasped.

"Why, thank you, ah, Willis."

"Wallace."

"I meant Wallace. And you are a very believable Schaunard."

He turned red and mumbled something.

I tried to put him at ease. "Have you sung the role often?"

"First time."

I could have guessed as much. When young artists are still learning roles, they study leads, not the minor parts. Wallace undoubtedly knew the role of Marcello, the baritone lead in *Bohème* that Scotti sang; I imagine he prayed every night for a stage light to fall on Scotti's head right before opening curtain.

Wallace was just beginning to loosen up and talk a little when Caruso returned—with Albert Oh-what-*is*-his-name? in tow. "Gerry, Gerry—do you know what this young scallion does?" Caruso sputtered.

"Rapscallion. What did he do?"

"He uses *Che gelida* for the warm-up!" Caruso's first-act aria in *Bohème*.

"But Mr. Caruso," Albert protested good-naturedly, "after hearing you sing it, it was the only music I could hear in my head!"

Caruso looked dubious. "Do you believe that?" he asked me.

I smiled. "One hundred percent."

"And if I were a soprano," Albert continued gallantly, "I'd be warming up with *Mi chiamano*." *My* first-act aria.

All this while Wallace had been glaring murderously at Albert, who hadn't so much as glanced at the young baritone. What a contrast between the two! Albert so outgoing and self-confident, Wallace so withdrawn and moody.

It was time for rehearsal to resume. But where was Scotti? The conductor sent a minion to find him.

He came back with both Scotti and the young soprano who was singing Musetta. Scotti was straightening his tie and the soprano was simpering; everyone in the room knew what had been going on. The young woman looked straight at me and smirked; *I can take him away from you if I want to. You and everything else in skirts, dearie.*

Nevertheless, I looked daggers at Scotti out of principle. Immediately he was at my side, contrite and attentive, full of compliments and *cara mia*s and a little hand-kissing thrown in for good measure. Dally he must; it was his nature. But he always returned to me. He just needed a little reminding once in a while, that's all.

We started the second act. The Musetta was a second- or third-generation immigrant named Olivia DiNardo who spoke with a Jersey accent but sang an impeccable Italian. She sailed through *Quando me'n vo' soletta* as if she'd been singing it all her life. And of course she sang full-voice, the show-off. Her top register was a bit wobbly, but she'd learn to control that in time.

Mimi doesn't have much to do in the second act, so I watched my two young admirers watching Olivia DiNardo. Of the three junior artists in the cast, she was the only one with a principal role. That put her a step above the other two, and they all knew it. Albert was better able to hide his resentment than Wallace was. Opera is *such* fun.

Caruso kept his word and played no practical jokes; I only hoped he wasn't saving them for the performance. The rehearsal proceeded, with no major hitches, through that heartbreaking trio in the third act up to Mimi's death in Act IV. Caruso stood over my lifeless body, and that golden voice cried out in despair the words that end the opera: "Mimi! . . . Mimi!" That "Mimi! . . . Mimi!" typifies everything about Italian opera that is exaggerated, melodramatic, contrived, overwrought, and mawkish—and I still get gooseflesh every time I hear it.

I also felt well satisfied; I'd be able to sing a good Mimi, I now knew. There was a tingle of anticipation in the air, the kind that comes only when artists know they're on the verge of an exciting performance. I accepted the congratulations of my fellow singers with pleasure.

Albert could have left after the second act, but he'd stayed to hear the rest of the rehearsal. Now he and Wallace were complimenting Olivia DiNardo, who accepted their good wishes like the prima donna she thought she already was. Then that audacious girl had the nerve to needle *me*.

"Oh, Miss Farrar," she said with the phoniest smile I have ever seen, "I just love the way you sing Mimi! All that emotion! It's so hard to know when *enough* becomes *too much* isn't it?"

"Not if you follow the music," I said. "It's all there."

"Still, I hope you don't listen to those who say sometimes you go too far. I just hope I can do as well when I take over the role. When I'm older, I mean." She cast a sidelong glance at Scotti.

Without missing a beat I said, "Olivia, you are going to make an outstanding Mimi." No irony, no sarcasm, no double meaning. Everyone listening got the point: she was catty, I was gracious. I had the pleasure of watching the young soprano turn red with embarrassment.

Well, one person missed the point; Caruso was oblivious to undertones. "No, no . . . Gerry, she is perfect Mimi. First time I hear her, in Monte Carlo—remember, Gerry?—I say, that is the Mimi Puccini dreams of when he writes *La Bohème*. Do I not say that, Gerry?"

"You certainly did, Rico."

Scotti sighed. "I was not there. I am devastated I do not hear your first Mimi, *cara mia*."

I rather liked the way the conversation was going. But then Wallace surprised everyone by saying, "Nobody ever notices baritones."

Scotti drew himself up to his full height. "*Some* baritones are noticed."

"But you're a star, Mr. Scotti," Wallace went on earnestly. "Among new singers, it's the sopranos and the tenors who get all the attention."

"That's true," said Albert insouciantly in his robust tenor.

I suddenly realized we were standing in two rows facing each other: Caruso, Scotti, and I—the stars—opposite the young tenor, baritone, and soprano who wanted to take our places. Like two armies facing off on a field of battle.

It was time to break this up. "Rehearsing always makes me hungry," I announced.

"It does?" Caruso said, undoubtedly wondering how he could have missed that all these years.

I moved over to the enemy line and linked arms with both Albert and Wallace. "So hungry, in fact, that I need *two* escorts to dinner. Well, gentlemen? Shall we go?"

"Oh, by all means!" Albert sang out joyously. Wallace smiled his shy smile and mumbled something.

"But, *carissima*—" Scotti started to protest.

"Not a word!" I commanded with a smile. Let him worry a little. The two boys were sweet, but they couldn't hold a candle to Scotti; he had a natural aristocratic bearing that gave him a *presence* the younger singers could only aspire to. But they had their charms, just the same, the younger ones; they made a nice change once in a while.

As we left I glanced back to see Olivia looking hopefully

at Scotti, but he didn't even notice. He just shook his head sadly after me and turned away, disconsolate at being alone for the evening.

Served him right.

I refused to continue.

Caruso had promised me—*promised* me—that he would be on his best behavior during the performance. Yet he couldn't wait until even the first act was over before playing one of his tricks. Right at the beginning of his *Che gelida manina*—"Your tiny hand is frozen . . ."—he'd put into my tiny hand a live mouse.

I'd dropped it immediately. It ran straight toward my long skirts, and the audience of the Metropolitan Opera was treated to the sight of the lead soprano doing an unrehearsed little dance that involved much shaking of skirts. All the while Caruso was singing away, having a rare old time laughing at my discomfiture.

And so that most tender of moments, the first meeting between the lovers-to-be, was ruined by a practical joke.

"The audience, they do not know what happens," Gatti-Casazza was saying in his most persuasive tones. "The mood, it is not spoiled. The duet goes beautifully—you hear the applause. They are ecstatic! They love you!"

"How could they *not* know what happened?" I objected.

"Because the moment is over almost as soon as it starts," he replied earnestly. "I myself am not sure what I see, it ends so quickly. Nothing is ruined, nothing is even damaged. You must finish the performance!"

"Not with that Neapolitan clown, I won't. This time he's gone too far. Gatti, he *knew* this was not just another performance for me."

"Yes, yes—you are right," he agreed hastily. "And Rico

knows he is wrong to hand you the mouse. He is most contrite!"

"Hah! Rico is always contrite. But that never stops him from doing it again."

"This time is different. I convince him his little joke is most unprofessional and he is eager to make amends. He waits outside—I send him in, yes?"

I didn't answer.

Gatti took that for assent and retreated. A moment later the door to my dressing room opened to admit Caruso.

He bent over, bared the back of his neck, and said: "There it is. Lop it off."

I tried not to laugh but it was impossible, he looked so ridiculous. But I gave him a tongue-lashing that made his ears burn. Caruso swore on the grave of every female ancestor whose name he could remember that there'd be no more tricks. He went down on his knees to apologize and ended up proposing marriage. The man was impossible.

Finally I told Gatti-Casazza that I'd finish the performance on one condition: that he personally search Caruso right before the tenor's every entrance. And if anything at all untoward happened from then on, I would walk off the stage.

Gatti searched him right then and there and found nothing concealed on his person except seven good-luck charms; Caruso was very superstitious. I declared myself satisfied, and Act II began.

It is a joyous, tuneful act; Albert came on for his brief moment in the spotlight and then disappeared offstage. But when it came time for the third-act trio, there was trouble: I found water on the stage floor in the spot where I am supposed to hide behind a tree.

Immediately I suspected Caruso. But I'd seen him

waiting offstage to make his entrance; when would he have done it? The stage was dry when the curtain opened.

Then the water rippled; it was dripping down from above. I looked up and saw a bucket perched on the top of the tree flat and held in place by a rope. Quickly I moved out of the way just as the rope jerked, the bucket tilted forward, and a rush of water came splashing down on the stage floor. At the same time a loud *thunk* sounded from backstage; something had fallen . . . the bucket?

A murmur of surprise rose from the audience, but I went on singing automatically as I tried to think. Caruso and Scotti were unaware that anything had happened; they were on the other side of the stage with their backs turned, and the orchestra drowned out the sound of the splash . . . but not the *thunk*. But seasoned professionals that they were, the two men paid no attention.

With an effort I put the distractions out of my mind and concentrated on the singing. By the time the trio was ended, we'd won the audience back; their applause was ear-shattering.

Caruso's practical jokes are idiotic and only occasionally funny. But dumping water on an artist *while she is performing* is just plain cruel. Caruso was not cruel.

Besides, somebody had to pull the rope to make the bucket spill.

Somehow we got through the rest of the act. We had to improvise our movements when Scotti and Caruso discovered the right side of the stage was unusable due to the unexplained deluge. As soon as the curtains closed, stagehands with mops ran out and got to work.

"I do not do it!" Caruso cried pathetically as accusing eyes turned on him.

Our general manager had stayed backstage to keep an

eye on Caruso, and now Gatti started lambasting the tenor, whose alarm at being accused of something he did not do was, in my opinion, quite genuine. Caruso was a poor dissembler; I could always tell when he was lying.

But before the accusations and denials had proceeded far, a scream cut through the babble of voices. There was much bewilderment and movement and uncertainty, until finally we got the word: one of the young artists had been found lying in a heap in the wings. Dead.

I followed the crowd to where one of the choristers had found the young singer. It was Albert. I was so shocked I could do nothing but stand there, hypnotized by the sight of his crumpled body. He'd evidently fallen from the stage right catwalk; his neck was broken. I stood there like a statue until Scotti came and gently led me away.

The next few minutes were nothing but confusion and noise. Gatti had the stagehands carry Albert's body to the greenroom; only then was I able to think again.

The catwalk Albert had fallen from was the only one from which it was possible to reach the tree flat that the bucket of water had been rigged to. *Albert* had tried to douse me with water? That made no sense. The only one in the cast who'd want to humiliate me was Olivia DiNardo.

A word with the stage manager revealed the fact that all three of our young artists had been watching the performance from the catwalk when they were not onstage. With my long skirts it was difficult, but I managed to climb up to the catwalk. It was unnerving up there . . . such a *long* way down. But yes: there was the bucket perched on a crossbrace across the top of the flat and tied into place. Someone standing on the downstage side of the catwalk need only tug on the rope attached to the handle to tip the bucket forward. One end of the rope trailed loosely over the catwalk railing. But that lovely bucket had to have a minute hole in the bottom, just enough for the dripping water to give me fair warning.

I tried to visualize Albert pulling such a trick, but I still couldn't see it. It had to be Olivia. So why was he the one to fall? Had he discovered what she was doing and tried to stop her?

Oh dear. Had she *pushed* him over the railing?

Then I noticed something caught on a nail in the wall. The light was poor up there, so I had to bend down to see. It was a piece of white cloth. I worked it loose and tucked it up my sleeve.

I made my way back down to the stage floor—more difficult, for some reason, than climbing up. Under a good light I examined my find: it was a plain cambric handkerchief, of the kind either a man or woman would carry. No embroidered "Olivia" to make my case. But there was something: strands of hemp caught in the threads. She'd wrapped the handkerchief around the rope to protect her hands from rope burn? Or Albert had. Or Wallace. No—it was Olivia, I was sure.

Gatti came lumbering up. "I look for you everywhere, Gerry," he said sorrowfully. "So dreadful that this happens during your return Mimi . . . we cancel, of course. That poor young man! So bright a future! We lose a potential star in Albert Gustafsson."

So his name was Gustafsson. "No," I said. "Don't cancel. We must finish the performance."

I'd never seen Gatti-Casazza gawk before, but he gawked then. "But you are the one who says—"

"I know what I said." The water bucket incident had been all but forgotten in the more serious business of Albert's death; I reminded Gatti. "Albert fell from the very spot where the bucket was rigged."

"Albert does this?"

"I don't think so. All three of the new singers were up there watching at various times. I think it was Olivia who put the bucket of water there, and I think Albert caught her at it."

"Olivia?!"

"She is the only one of the three who would wish to embarrass me." I showed him the handkerchief I'd found with its strands of hemp caught in the threads.

Gatti thought a minute. "You stand by the tree during the trio. But later, first Scotti and then Caruso are there. Briefly, but they at least pass through the spot."

He was right; I hadn't thought of that. "You mean one of the boys could have been out to douse Caruso or Scotti? But no—the bucket tipped while *I* was standing there."

"If there is a struggle up on the catwalk . . ."

". . . then the bucket might have been tipped prematurely?" I still believed it was Olivia, but he had a point. "All the more reason for continuing the performance. It will give us a chance to see which one of them claims the handkerchief, Olivia or Wallace. I can leave it on the stage during the performance."

"And if neither of them claims it?"

I shrugged. "Then it was Albert? I don't know. Let's try the handkerchief and see what happens."

The audience out front was growing restless. It had been far too long an intermission, and the stage set wasn't even changed yet. Gatti sent his assistant out in front of the curtain to announce there'd been an accident backstage but everything was under control now and the performance would resume shortly and thank you for your patience.

We all hurried around getting ready for the last act.

Shortly before the curtain was to open, I slipped on to the stage and dropped the handkerchief on the floor right under the offending catwalk. I was very tense; even though I was convinced it was Olivia who was the cause of Albert's death, to be fair I ought to keep an eye on Wallace as well. But I couldn't watch both of them *and* the conductor *and* the man in the prompt box all at the same time; I needed help.

I enlisted Scotti's aid. I had to repeat a few things before he took it all in. "You want me to watch Wallace? *Per dio!* I watch him like the hawk. How dare he try to make me look foolish?"

"It wasn't Wallace," I disagreed. "It was Olivia. But watch him anyway."

"*Cara mia,* I know Wallace is your pet, but—"

"It's not that. Which of those two has the aggression and the nerve to pull a stunt like that? Wallace is a shrinking violet."

Scotti shook his head. "Still waters run smooth."

"They run deep, but I don't think that's the case here."

A harried-looking little man ran up to us. "Mr. Scotti, *please!* We're ready to start!" Scotti took his place on stage with Caruso, and Act IV at last began.

I entered with Olivia in this act. We stood by the upstage entrance awaiting our cue, avoiding each other's eyes and not speaking. Olivia's cue came; she entered, sang her few lines, and then came back to get me. I slumped against her; she wrapped both arms around me and helped me drag my poor dying body onstage.

It was a strange performance; dying convincingly isn't easy under the best of circumstances, but I had to do it without letting Olivia out of my sight. Scotti's idea of watching Wallace was to stand so close to him that he was breathing down the young man's neck. But I didn't have to maintain my vigil long; the minute Olivia spotted the handkerchief, she scooped it up and tucked it into her pocket.

I was right.

Oh, what a relief! From that point on I gave myself up totally to the business of expiring as melodically as I could. Caruso's ringing tones sang out "Mimi! . . . Mimi!"; the curtain closed; I leapt from my deathbed and sprang at Olivia DiNardo.

Alas, she was physically stronger than I, and I was getting the worse of it when without a moment's thought Caruso jumped into the fray. Between the two of us, we wrestled her to the floor.

"Gerry," Caruso said, panting, "why do we fight with this young lady?"

"She's responsible for Albert's death," I told him. "Hold her, Rico!"

He got her to her feet and wrapped two beefy arms around her from the rear. I pulled the handkerchief out of her pocket and held it under her nose. "You wrapped this around the rope tied to the bucket—to protect your hands. Don't deny it!" She started boo-hooing.

Gatti hurried on to the stage. "It is Olivia?"

"It is indeed. Better call the police."

"The *police!*" she shrieked. "You never call the police when *Caruso* plays a practical joke!"

The audience out front was applauding thunderously. "Curtain call!" the stage manager yelled frantically. "Curtain call!" Gatti sent Wallace and another secondary singer out to take their bows.

"Yes, the police," I said to Olivia. "Not for trying to dump water on me during a performance, although that should be punishable by at least ten years in prison. But for causing Albert's death." Fresh tears from Olivia. "You pushed him off the catwalk, didn't you?"

"I did not push him!" she screamed.

The stage manager cried, "Mr. Scotti . . . curtain call!"

For the first time in his life, Scotti didn't want to leave to take a bow. But Gatti pushed him toward where the stage manager was holding the curtain open.

"If you didn't push him," I said to Olivia, "then why is Albert dead?"

"Gerry," Caruso said, "my arms—they tire."

"Let her go." He released her. "Well, Olivia?"

"It was an accident," she wailed. "I didn't want to hurt him! He was trying to stop me—you know, the bucket? Oh, Miss Farrar, I'm so sorry! I don't know what got into me, it's just, I don't know, you have everything I want for myself and—"

"Nobody cares about that," I said sharply. "Tell us about Albert."

"Miss Farrar!" the stage manager bellowed. "Curtain call!"

"Not now!" I snapped.

"I go," Caruso said and trotted toward the opening in the curtain.

"Albert found me on the catwalk holding the rope," Olivia said between sobs. "He tried to take the rope away from me and I was trying to elbow him back, and I got flustered and pulled the rope too soon, and, and, I guess he just leaned too far over the railing. He didn't make a sound as he went down—it was so *fast!* I wasn't even sure what had happened until I heard him hit. But I didn't push him! Do you really think I'd *kill* somebody just to keep it quiet about, you know, the bucket?"

Put that way . . . it did seem improbable. Exposure as a

practical joker, even a cruel one, was not cause for murder. It was just a stupid accident, but an accident *she* had had a hand in causing. Poor Albert had plummeted to his death trying to prevent me from being humiliated on stage. I would gladly have taken the soaking if that would have kept him alive.

Gatti-Casazza planted himself in front of Olivia. "I do not know what the police do with you. But I tell you this. You never sing on the stage of this opera house again. Never! Do you hear? Never!"

She burst into tears again—sincere ones, this time. Gatti grasped her firmly by the arm and led her off the stage.

Caruso had milked his curtain call as long as he could, but now he was back. "She confesses?" he wanted to know.

"In a way," I said.

Scotti took my hand and patted it. "You do good, *cara mia.*"

I smiled at them both, glad it was all over. Then I went out to take my curtain call.

"Stet"—a word every author has scribbled far too many times—is a story written for a British mystery anthology featuring women protagonists who have some connection with books or publishing. A big change has taken place in mystery publishing; the tough-talking, trenchcoat-wearing, hardboiled private eye was—for a while, at least—pretty much pushed out of the market by the new generation of female investigators. My protagonist is an editor who runs into some unpleasant backlash against that change.

STET

Julia Cutler stared gloomily at the edited manuscript on her desk. She'd flipped through the pages to see how many times the word "stet" had been written in the righthand margins; there was at least one on every page, frequently as many as six.

Some writers couldn't *stand* to be edited.

Martin Klein was one such. Martin was a shallow writer, but until recently a popular one; his books were action-filled and entertaining in an old-fashioned macho sort of way. His mystery plots were full of holes; and he had a stable of about six characters he drew upon regularly, changing their names from book to book. Still, as long as his books kept selling, Julia would keep buying them for Gotham House.

But even that was becoming problematic; Martin Klein's last two books had been disappointing, with fewer sales and higher returns than ever before. The kind of book Martin wrote had been in decline for years, and Julia was vaguely surprised that he'd managed to hold on as long as he had. The handwriting was on the wall, though.

With a sigh she got to work. Her rule of thumb was to give the writer his or her way in every instance that was not an outright violation of usage, spelling, or factual accuracy. But Martin tended to get sloppy about grammar—right there was an example: "She was one of those women who always has to have the last word." The copyeditor had correctly changed "has" to "have"; but Martin had written a big red "stet" in the margin—let it stand as it is. Julia drew two blue lines through the "stet".

It was dark and the other Gotham employees had gone home by the time Julia finished. Martin's new book was called *Swimming in Blood*; the word *Blood* appeared in every Martin Klein title. Another Martin Klein trademark was an extended scene in which his private-eye hero got beat to a pulp. Usually the scene appeared about halfway through the book so Martin could show his hero struggling valiantly on even though in great pain. Real he-man.

Julia had meant to run a couple of errands before she met Dan for dinner, but there wasn't time now. She wrapped up warm against New York's harsh January winds and took a cab to Three-Card Monty's on Fifty-seventh Street. Dan was sitting in the bar area, waiting for her.

Julia sank down on the bar stool beside him. "Martini," she told the bartender.

Dan grinned and said, "No need to ask what kind of day you had. What happened?"

"Martin Klein's new book happened, that's what." The bartender brought her martini and she took a sip. "No real problems—just tedious work."

Dan grinned. "And does good old Whatsisname get the stuffing knocked out of him again?"

Martin's fictional detective. "Of course he does," Julia replied with a smile. "And of course Martin won't allow a word of his precious prose to be changed. So, what about you? Catch any bad guys today?"

Dan Bernhard was a police detective working out of New York's Midtown South Precinct. He claimed Midtown South was too big a precinct for only twenty-three detectives to cover; moreover, he didn't like his lieutenant and he had little respect for his partner. Still, he insisted he liked police work. Julia didn't know him well enough yet to question him on the point.

She listened carefully as he told her about a new gang war that had broken out in the project houses along FDR Drive and was spreading uptown. It was a territorial thing, Dan said. Who had the right to sell drugs on what streets. America's Future Lies in Its Youth.

It was a depressing subject, but Julia didn't have to fake an interest. Like everyone connected with mystery writing, she had a certain degree of curiosity about police work. Dan was a bright, college-educated go-getter who'd been partnered with an old-time street-tough cop who was barely literate. The two men tended to look down on each other, not an easy situation.

They went into the dining room and ordered. Julia couldn't imagine doing the kind of work Dan did and still remain a nice guy, but somehow Dan had managed it. They'd met when Gotham House had been broken into the previous week and Dan and his partner had been sent to investigate. One computer had been taken, nothing else. The thief had not been caught.

Dan was still thinking of Martin Klein and his fictional

detective. "The trouble with Klein's books, he always makes the police out to be stupid or corrupt or both. I haven't read all his stuff—did he ever write a cop who was good at his job?"

"Not that I recall."

"I'd like to see him spend a couple of days in Midtown South and learn something about how cops really operate. Open his eyes a little."

"It'll never happen," Julia said with a rueful smile. "Martin's writing a fantasy series—one strong man taking on the establishment and always coming out on top. A series like that can't stand very much reality. He makes the cops stupid because he doesn't know any other way to make his private investigator look smart. Martin's hardboiled detective is an anachronism."

"Then why do you publish the books?" Dan asked—and laughed at the expression on her face. "I know, I know. Money. But doesn't it bother you?"

"I can't afford to let it bother me," she said crisply, not quite yet willing to admit that Klein's days with Gotham House were coming to an end. "And you'd be surprised at the number of people who take Martin Klein seriously. There's someone in Texas writing a Master's thesis about him right now."

"Good God. But why? What's the appeal? Why do people read junk like that?"

"Don't ask me," Julia replied. "I'm only his editor."

At that point they dropped the subject and enjoyed their dinner.

Gotham House published a number of authors like Martin Klein, less-than-Nobel-quality writers whose sales kept Gotham in business. Taken as a whole, they even brought in enough money to let Julia take a chance on an unknown writer now and then.

The next morning Julia eyed the stack of manuscripts on her desk that had made it past the first readers. The stack had been there for ten days; she couldn't put it off any longer. *Editors don't read manuscripts,* Julia thought gloomily; *they just talk on the phone and go to meetings.* But her first meeting wasn't until two that afternoon, and the telephone was strangely silent.

She spread out the manuscripts and skimmed through the readers' evaluations. The sixth one she came to made her pause. It was a rave. That was unusual, made even more so by the fact that the evaluation had been written by Rosemary Vance . . . who never raved. Ever. Rosemary was Julia's editorial assistant who helped out with the slush pile when she could, and she'd turned out to be Julia's hardest-to-please reader. But she'd been pleased this time. "A new female investigator," Rosemary had written, "that will put all the others to shame. With the proper promotion, we could have a bestseller here." She'd gone on about the author's lively style, her sense of humor, even her humanity.

Julia felt a stir of excitement. She opened the manuscript and began to read.

And was appalled.

The heroine spent the first three pages worrying about her appearance. By the end of the first chapter she'd gotten herself into a spot of trouble that required her rescue by a stalwart boyfriend. She'd inherited her father's detective agency but didn't want to do investigative work; what she really wanted was a home and babies and a strong man to take care of her.

Julia read on. This new female detective that was supposed to set the world on fire conducted an investigation based solely on hunches and wild guesses. When she discovered a dead body, she fainted. Julia glanced again at Rosemary Vance's neatly typed evaluation sheet: "A new, sensitive woman detective just in time for the new century."

This was the wave of the future? More like a retreat to the fifties. Julia leaned back in her chair and tried to think. The story wasn't meant to be a parody, she was certain of that. The name on the manuscript was Amanda Forrest, a name unknown to Julia, as were all of the names on the unsolicited manuscripts that came to her office.

Amanda Forrest, whoever she was, was a throwback. But what had Rosemary seen in that manuscript that made her think it was a winner? Only one way to find out. She pressed the button hand-labeled "Rosemary" on the phone.

And got the voice-message service. Annoyed, Julia went looking for her. And found that no one had seen her assistant that morning. Had she called in sick? No one knew.

Her annoyance giving way to concern, Julia dialed Rosemary Vance's home number but reached only the answering machine in the apartment in the Village that Rosemary shared with two other young women. Julia looked up Rosemary's cell phone number and called that.

It rang four times and then a male voice answered. Julia could hear street noises in the background. "Yeah?" the voice said.

Somebody else had her phone? "I want to talk to Rosemary," Julia said almost belligerently.

"Who's calling?"

"Julia Cutler. Who's this?"

"Julia! It's Dan Bernhard. Who was it you wanted to talk to?"

Dan? "My assistant, Rosemary Vance. Why—"

"Describe her."

"Dan, what's going on?"

"Please—Describe her."

Julia took a deep breath. "She's twenty-five years old, about five-four or -five, a bit on the plump side. She has thick, shiny black hair that she wears very short."

There was a brief silence. Then Dan said, "I'm afraid I've got bad news."

Julia listened in horror as Dan explained that her assistant had been stabbed and killed. Her body had been found in a dumpster behind a café on Fourteenth Street. No purse near the body, so they hadn't known her name until Julia called. Rosemary had been wearing her cell phone clipped to her belt under her coat, so the killer hadn't seen that. Dan wanted to know if Rosemary Vance had any family in New York.

"Ah, no," Julia said, trying to marshal her thoughts. "She came here from Iowa. She was mugged? She was killed by a mugger?"

"No family," Dan went on. "Then I'm going to have to ask you to do something. We need a positive ID. That means viewing the body, Julia. They're taking her away now, so could you come down to the morgue? The sooner the better. Can you do that?"

Julia stammered out agreement, and forced herself to focus while Dan told her how to find the city mortuary on First Avenue. She hung up and just sat staring at nothing, trying to absorb the news.

She was still sitting like that when a familiar voice rang out, "Ah, there she is, the dishiest editor in New York! Do I have a proposition for—God, Julia, what's the matter? You're white as a sheet!"

Not for the first time Julia wished that Martin Klein lived in Hawaii or some place equally far away. Stocky, short neck, a face he liked to describe as "lived-in"—Martin seemed to take up three-fourths of the space in her office. "I've just been talking to the police," Julia said. She explained about Rosemary Vance and watched his mouth work wordlessly as he tried to take in what she was telling him.

Finally he said, "Rosemary? Rosemary's dead?" He swore. "A mugging! When did this happen?"

Julia stood up and got her coat. "I don't know, Martin. But I have to go down to the morgue now. They need someone to make a formal identification."

Martin gave himself a little shake and said, "I'll go for you. That's no job for a woman."

She bit back a retort; he was trying to help. "Thanks, but they're expecting me."

"Then I'm coming with you. Don't argue, now."

She didn't. For once, Julia didn't mind Martin Klein's company.

It was even worse than she'd thought, looking through the glass window at Rosemary lying on that gurney, so obviously naked beneath the concealing sheet. Julia and Martin both identified her quickly and left the room.

Dan Bernhard followed them out to the hallway in the city mortuary, along with his partner, a fiftyish cop named Finelli who had a strangely oversized head. Dan murmured a few perfunctory words of condolence and asked, "Do you know if she had any enemies?"

"Enemies?" Martin exclaimed. "Wasn't she killed by a mugger?"

Finelli shook his big head. "That wasn't no mugging. Muggers don't hang around and try to hide their victims. Perp took the purse to make it look like a mugging."

Another shock. "Why would anyone want to kill Rose-mary?" Julia protested.

"That's what we're trying to find out, lady. *Did* she have any enemies?"

"Not in the office," Julia answered. "I don't know about her private life. Her roommates could tell you—she shared an apartment with two other girls."

"Got an address?"

Julia told him the number on Bleecker Street. "When was she killed?"

"Couple hours ago," Finelli answered. "She goes into the caf for breakfast, she goes out, and . . . *zap!* Somebody lets her have it."

Dan promised to keep her informed. The cab ride back uptown to Gotham House was a silent one, both Julia and Martin lost in their own thoughts.

But she was surprised when Martin didn't get out of the cab. "Aren't you coming up?"

"I don't think this is the best time to pitch an idea," he said. "I'll come back in a few days."

Julia hesitated. "I think I need something new to concen-trate on, right now. Come tell me what your idea is."

It was an invitation she was soon to regret. Martin wanted to edit an anthology of short stories based on var-ious characters in his books, all the stories to be written by other writers. Julia wasn't enamored of the idea; character-ization wasn't Martin's strong point.

His eyes were glittering with what Julia at first thought was eagerness but soon recognized as desperation. Martin started talking more and more rapidly, dropping names of bestselling mystery writers he claimed he could get to con-tribute to the anthology . . . as if Lawrence Block or Sara Paretsky would put their own work on hold to write about

Martin Klein's cardboard characters. Martin wasn't stupid; he could see his series was in trouble. So he'd come up with this cockamamie scheme to keep interest alive by recruiting good writers to do his work for him. Julia finally got rid of him by promising to bring the matter up at the next sales meeting.

Not much work got done at Gotham the rest of that day. Julia had to force herself to inform the rest of the staff of what had happened to Rosemary Vance; inviting Martin Klein up had been a delaying tactic. Following the same stunned disbelief that Julia herself had felt when she first heard the news, all the members of the staff had questions, questions that Julia didn't know the answers to.

She met Dan for a quick drink after work. "We haven't learned a damned thing," he told her. "She had breakfast alone, read the *Times* while she was eating. Nobody saw anything, of course . . . they never do. Medical examiner says she was killed by a long, thick blade—a stiletto. Her roommates don't know nuttin' about nuttin', as Finelli says. Vance had no boyfriend at the moment, no financial problems outside the usual, and her health was okay."

"So what do you do now?"

"Have another go at the roommates. Lieutenant Larch is already hollering at us to put this one away."

The lieutenant that he disliked. "After only one day?"

"Yeah, well, most killings are nailed down right away or not at all. She doesn't like long investigations."

"She?"

"Yup. Our lady lieutenant." Dan laughed shortly. "Who just loves to give orders. Oh boy, does she love to give orders! Bossiest broad I ever met."

Julia didn't care for what she was hearing. "And you don't like taking orders . . . from a woman?"

"Oh, hey, come on, Julia! I don't like taking orders from *that* woman. And I'm sorry I said 'broad'—okay?"

They smiled and talked of other things, but neither of them was comfortable after that. They finished their drinks and went their separate ways.

Julia finished the soup she'd picked up at a deli and opened her briefcase. Inside was a manuscript: *Flowering Evil*, by Amanda Forrest. Julia had given the book only a hasty reading, and an incomplete one; she'd quit after Chapter 4. But *Flowering Evil* was the last book Rosemary Vance had recommended before she died, and it deserved a good, close reading because of that. Julia settled down to work.

It wasn't until Chapter 6 that Julia began to suspect the truth. One sentence read: "He was one of those men who always has to be right"—an all-too-familiar verb error. Certain other turns of phrases sounded familiar as well. She'd seen some of the characters before, using different names in a different set of books. Julia wondered whether the heroine would get beat to a pulp halfway through the book.

She did. In Chapter 13.

He wasn't even a good enough writer to disguise his style; but what capped it for Julia was the fact that at the end of the manuscript, "Amanda Forrest" had attached a sheet proposing further books in the series—*Flowering Avarice*, *Flowering Violence*, *Flowering Lust*. The same naming gimmick he'd used in his hardboiled series (and not an original one at that).

Julia had underestimated the extent of Martin Klein's desperation; she should have seen it coming. The mystery field was once dominated by men—men got the bigger advances, the bigger cut of the advertising pie, the more reviews. The women, for the most part, had to take the scraps. Then came the Revolution, and the new spate of female investigators that appeared on the scene had pretty much pushed the old-fashioned, trench-coated, tough-talking male private eye right out of the market. There were a few years there when no new male detectives at all were introduced to the reading public; they were poison at the bookstores. Many of the men writers were resentful, never sparing a thought for how the women had felt all those years when *they* had been shut out.

A few of the well-established older series had managed to hang on, Martin Klein's among them. But Martin had understood his time too was drawing to an end, so . . . if you can't lick 'em, join 'em. But whatever had made him think he could write from a woman's point of view? A lot of men could—but not Martin Klein. All the women in Martin's books were either evil temptresses or helpless victims, Delilah or Little Nell.

But where did Rosemary Vance fit into all this? Rosemary was a sharp reader; she would have recognized Martin's style just as quickly as Julia had. Yet Rosemary had written that glowing evaluation; had Martin gotten to her and bribed her? Julia couldn't believe that; for one thing, Rosemary could be stubborn and self-righteous about even the most minor things—a point of grammar, for instance. Rosemary Vance, Julia thought, had probably been the most *un*bribable member of the Gotham House staff.

Oh, what a mess. Julia gave it up for the night and went to bed.

Dan Bernhard manned one desk in an open squadroom on the second floor of the Midtown South stationhouse on West Thirty-fifth. The place was busy and the noise level just short of deafening. A couple of homeboys who'd been arrested—at nine in the morning?—were mouthing off at the detectives leading them none too gently to an interrogation room. The phones never stopped ringing. Julia caught a glimpse of the lieutenant Dan disliked; she was just an ordinary-looking woman, one who gave away nothing about herself.

Dan's partner was sitting at the desk facing Dan's. "So you're saying this Martin Klein killed Rosemary Vance? Because she didn't like his book?" The skepticism was heavy in Finelli's voice.

"It's more than that," Julia said. "His livelihood's at stake."

Dan picked up the evaluation sheet for *Flowering Evil*. "She says here that the book's a winner."

"If she wrote that. I don't think she did." Julia sighed. "That just isn't her language, Dan. Rosemary wouldn't be that enthusiastic even about a good book, and *Flowering Evil*, well . . ."

"It sucks."

"Does it ever."

"So Martin Klein wrote this evaluation himself? And somehow substituted it for the one Rosemary wrote?"

Julia nodded. "Remember the break-in we had last week—when the computer was stolen? That must have been Martin, sneaking in to substitute his own evaluation for Rosemary's. He'd have taken the computer to account for the jimmied door."

Finelli frowned. "And Rosemary was there working late? She caught him in the act?"

"I don't think so. She would have said something to me."

Finelli snorted. "He bought her off."

"You don't know she was even there!" Julia flared.

"That break-in . . ."—Dan was counting back—". . . that was eight days ago. Where's the evaluation sheet been all this time? And the manuscript?"

Julia smiled wryly. "On my desk. Waiting to be read."

He picked up the manuscript. "*Flowering Evil.* Cribbed from Baudelaire?"

"Who?" Finelli said.

Dan ignored him. "Julia, are you absolutely certain this book was written by Martin Klein?"

"Yes, absolutely."

Finelli's big head wagged back and forth. "It'll never stand up in court."

"It's admissible," Dan said quickly. "Expert testimony."

Finelli wasn't buying it. "That ain't *real* evidence. The way a guy writes. Shee-ut."

So scornful. "Look, Detective Finelli," Julia said. "I know this isn't the kind of detective work you do every day, but it *is* detective work. I see the clues, and I recognize the style. I can go through that manuscript page by page and show you parallels to Martin Klein's other books."

"You may have to," Finelli muttered.

Dan shrugged. "If that's what it takes."

"Yeah, but will a jury believe her? You know what the lieutenant'll say if we go to her with this kinda evidence, Danny Boy."

His partner shot him a sharp look and turned back to Julia. "There's one way we can get Klein. We put a wire on you."

Julia's eyes widened. "I go meet him alone while you sit in a place of safety and listen in? No, thank you. I've read too many books where too many dumb heroines confront killers alone."

"You won't be alone," Dan said hastily. "Klein doesn't

know us—we'll be right there in plain sight. You can meet him in some public place. A restaurant. This is a team effort, Julia. You help us, we help you."

"But I don't *know* that he killed Rosemary!"

"Then mebbe we eliminate him as a suspect," Finelli said. "Either way, we learn something."

"It's the only way to be sure," Dan added.

Reluctantly, Julia agreed. "But how can I get him to give himself away? I can't just come right out and ask him."

Dan loosened his tie. "That's what we need to figure out right now."

La Feria was a Peruvian shop/eatery on Broadway. The shop took up all the ground floor area and sold only small items—some Peruvian apparel, painted trays, colorful knick-knacks. Overlooking the shop was a balcony housing a small dining area and, at the rear, a bar. Julia's table was at the frontmost part of the balcony where she was visible from the street through the two-story glass front, about as "public" as she could get. Dan was sitting at the bar; Finelli was at a nearby table demolishing a plate of *ropa vieja*. Outside in a parked car were two other detectives who'd record everything she and Martin Klein said.

From her table by the wrought-iron balcony railing Julia could see Martin enter the shop area and head for the open staircase. He looked up and saw her and put on a big artificial smile. Julia clasped her hands in her lap to hide her nervousness.

"I hope this summons to lunch means good news," Martin said as he sat down.

"In a way," Julia responded noncommittally. "Let's order first." They spent a minute studying the menu and gave their orders to the waitress.

Julia took the manuscript of *Flowering Evil* out of her briefcase and put it on the table. A tic appeared in Martin's cheek, but he made a show of reading the title page. "Amanda Forrest? One of your new discoveries?"

"One of Rosemary's discoveries. I don't think the book's much good, myself. But Rosemary wrote a glowing evaluation . . . and since it's the last book she recommended, I want to give it a chance. It needs a professional hand, though, and I thought of you. The rewrite should be a breeze, and you'd get a nice hunk of the royalties."

It had been Julia's idea to throw Martin off-balance by asking him to rewrite himself—and now she watched as he struggled to keep his composure. "I don't do rewrites."

"I know, but I thought you might make an exception in this case. At least read the manuscript."

He decided to bluff. "What is it, some pushy female investigator who needs to be rescued every other chapter?"

Julia leaned forward in her chair. "How did you know she needed to be rescued?"

"Well, they all do, don't they?"

"No, Martin, as a matter of fact they don't. Female private investigators are able to take care of themselves. Haven't you read any of the women's P.I. books? You should have done your homework before you tried to cash in."

"What!?"

"I know you wrote *Flowering Evil*, Martin. And I think Rosemary knew it too."

The waitress arrived with their food; her two customers stared at each other without speaking until she'd left. "You're out of your mind!" Martin hissed.

"Oh, stop it!" Julia said impatiently. "I'm prepared to offer you a deal, but I can't if you go on claiming to know nothing about *Flowering Evil*."

He looked at her skeptically. "What kind of deal?"

"I'm willing to let you get away with this pretense in exchange for fifty percent of the advance and the royalties. The series will be controversial, because it's so obviously written by a misogynist. We milk that controversy for all it's worth and split the take right down the middle. You write the stuff, I'll see that it gets published and promoted."

"Fifty percent!"

"Which leaves you with fifty. As opposed to the zero percent you'll have otherwise. You can try taking that piece of crap to other publishers if you like. But I can tell you what will happen—they'll laugh you out of the office. No, Martin, it's Gotham House or nothing. That's the deal."

A small smile appeared on Martin's face. "Well, well. So Queen Julia is on the take. Whoever would have thought it?" He was silent a moment. Then: "Very well, I accept your deal."

Julia saw Finelli get up from his table and go downstairs to the shop area; through the front window she could see it had started snowing. Dan was still at the bar, carefully not watching them. Julia said to Martin, "But first, you have to tell me about Rosemary."

"I don't know anything about what happened to Rosemary!" he protested.

"Then the deal's off. I've got to know what I'm getting into here."

He stared. "You're joking."

Julia looked down at her untasted lunch. "She figured out you had written *Flowering Evil*. Did she call you? She didn't say anything about it to me."

"Yes, she called me." Martin made a sound of exasperation. "She was working late—you and everyone else had gone home. That bitch took a great deal of pleasure in reading me the evaluation she'd just written. Then she oh-so-sweetly advised me not to try writing from a woman's point of view again. She said I 'didn't have a clue'." His face darkened. "Rosemary never did appreciate my work. It was just my luck that *she* should be the one to read *Flowering Evil.*"

"So you broke into our office later that same night—to substitute your own evaluation for Rosemary's? And stole a computer to account for the break-in?"

He looked surprised that she'd figured that part out. "There was no talking sense to Rosemary, you know, once she'd made up her mind. Pig-headed young woman. I found the manuscript on your desk, with the evaluation sheet clipped to it. I made the switch and put the manuscript about halfway down the stack."

"But surely you knew Rosemary would speak up when—"

"It was a stop-gap measure, Julia, for Christ's sake!" he snapped . . . and then remembered to lower his voice. "Of course I knew I had to do something about Rosemary. She was standing between me and publication."

Julia's mouth dropped open. "You were that sure I would buy the book?"

Martin shrugged. "You've always bought my books before. Look under the table."

"What?"

"Look under the table."

Wondering, Julia bent sideways and looked . . . and saw a long knife clasped in Martin's hand. Slowly, she sat back up. She cast a sidelong glance at the bar.

Dan wasn't there.

Stay calm. For the benefit of the microphone taped to her breastbone, she said, "You have a knife. A *long* knife. Are you going to kill me too, Martin?"

"I'm hoping I won't have to," he said. "I was able to keep Rosemary quiet for a few days by scaring her—she didn't like the sight of a stiletto any more than you do. But I was losing her. It was only a matter of time before she told you what was going on. But you—you're an even bigger danger than she was."

"I offered you a deal," Julia said quickly. "I'm willing to stick by it."

He snorted. "I'll bet you are." He looked around; every table in the dining area was filled. "Leave some money on the table and put your coat on."

"Where are we going?"

"Someplace less public."

Even with Dan and Finelli mysteriously gone, Julia knew she was safer right where she was. "No. I won't do it." Suddenly she felt a sharp pain in her left knee that made her gasp.

"That was just a sample," Martin said. "Remember, a knife doesn't make a noise when it goes off. Don't make me kill you, Julia. I need to think. Get up—we're leaving."

She did as he said. When she stood up, she saw a red spot on the left knee of her pants. Going down the stairway, she glanced around the shop area but couldn't spot either Dan or Finelli.

Outside, she turned the collar of her coat up against the wind; Martin grasped one arm and held her close beside him. There was an air of unreality about the scene; the gray sky, the swirling snowflakes, the pedestrians hurrying by with their eyes on their feet—none of it seemed to have anything to do with her. *Is this how Rosemary felt the last moments of her life?*

"You know the drill," Martin muttered. "One false move and you're dead, sister." He waved at a cab that sped right on by.

In spite of the danger, the editor in her couldn't help thinking: *What dreadful dialogue.* "What turned you into a killer, Martin?"

"You did. You and your kind. You women have taken over everything. All the editors are women now. Who the hell do you think you are? You couldn't write a book if your life depended on it, yet *you* decide whether *I* get published or not."

Julia saw red. "So it's all *my* fault?"

"You're spoiling everything. Why couldn't you just let things stand the way they were? Taxi!"

This time a cab stopped. Martin dragged her into the street, but Julia was so outraged she could barely see where she was walking. "I will not be your scapegoat!" she yelled.

"Shut up! And get in!"

"I'm not getting into that cab with you!" The cab driver, seeing what looked like a fight about to break out, hit the gas pedal and sped away. With a cry Julia twisted around and kicked Martin as hard as she could behind his knees.

His knees buckled and he went down flat on his back. Without stopping to think, Julia flung herself full-length on top of him. She knew she wouldn't be able to hold him down, but it was all she could think to do.

"He's got a knife!" a passerby cried out.

"Nemmind, I got it," a familiar voice said. A big foot stepped on Martin's wrist and Finelli twisted the stiletto out of his grasp. "Okay, Superwoman, you can let him up now."

Julia scrambled to her feet. "Geez, Finelli, where were you?"

"In the Peruvian shop—where you couldn't see me." He hauled a swearing Martin to his feet and turned him over to two men Julia didn't know, presumably the detectives who'd been recording everything. Finelli said, "Why dincha just run, when you knocked him down?"

She shrugged. "Where would that get me?"

He gave her a lopsided grin. "You're fierce when you're riled."

Uh-huh. "Where's Dan?"

As if on cue, Dan came bursting out through the doors. "Julia? Finelli? What happened?"

"We got 'im," Finelli snarled, "no thanks to you. Where the hell you been? It wasn't supposed to go this far. What if she'd gotten into a cab with him? Where were you?"

"Uh, I had to answer a call of nature."

"You couldn't hold it, fer Chrissake?" Finelli was disgusted. "How can I depend on a partner who endangers a civilian because he has to go pee?"

"Put a cork in it, Finelli," Dan said testily. He turned to Julia. "Are you all right?"

No thanks to you. "Whatever happened to the team effort?" she asked. "I help you, you help me."

He wouldn't meet her eye. "Yeah, well, you know how it goes, team effort. Sometimes it doesn't work out."

"I've noticed that." *Not even an apology.*

"Thanks for your help," Finelli said to her.

"And for yours." She meant it.

"It wasn't as if I left you on your own," Dan said. "Finelli was there, and you did all right."

Excuses? Julia looked him straight in the eye. "Goodbye, Dan."

He didn't try to stop her as she walked away.

A Christmas story—well, a story set at Christmastime. One that could have been titled "Too Many Santas". A story that revels in the spirit of the season, jingle bells, jolly old elves, twinkling Christmas tree lights, good will toward men, murder, like that. Ho ho ho.

HO HO HO

"He used to be Santa Claus," the store manager said.

"Used to be," Sergeant Murphy repeated.

"Until he was promoted. Now he trains all our Santas. Or did train them, I should say."

The two stood looking down at the fat man lying spread-eagle on the floor. "How many Santas do you have?" the police sergeant asked.

"Two for the main store and two for each of the four branches, plus three on standby. That's thirteen altogether."

"So any one of thirteen could have killed him."

The store manager sighed. "So it would appear."

The dead man was named Harvey Nye. He was about fifty, weighed over two hundred pounds, and was dressed in sweats and Reeboks. A burly man, thick-necked and big-shouldered. But that thick neck hadn't protected him; he'd been strangled with a string of Christmas tree lights, which, grotesquely, had then been plugged into a nearby socket. Nye's seasonal garrote blinked on and off, on and off. The ex-Santa had died clutching a fake white beard in his right hand, a scrap of red cloth in his left. "Who found the body?" Sergeant Murphy asked.

"Santa Number Five. They were just coming back from their morning break, you see, and Number Five was first into the room."

The room was located on the ninth floor of Biedermann's Department Store and had been set up as a classroom. Christmas decorations ornamented the windowless walls, and in the corner sat a small tree—without its lights. "You number your Santas?" Sergeant Murphy asked.

"Harvey did. He said it made it easier to call on them during the three-day training session."

Sergeant Murphy told the store manager he could go. The Crime Scene Unit came in and took pictures of Harvey Nye and his necklace of twinkling lights. When the body was finally removed, Murphy sent for the Santa Clauses. They came bouncing in, thirteen jolly old elves that jingled as they walked, ushered along by two police officers who then stationed themselves on both sides of the door. The Santas were a mixture of retired older men, college students looking to make a few bucks for Christmas, unemployed men taking anything they could get, and one or two who just liked playing Santa. They were all corpulent, either naturally or with the aid of padding, and they were all in costume and wearing numbered placards pinned to the fronts of their suits. "Hee hee hee!" Santa Number Ten was snickering. "Somebuddy decorated old Harvey."

Number Five growled. "Show some respect for the dead!"

"Why?" Number Ten asked reasonably. "Nobuddy respected him alive."

"Ain't that the truth," Number Four chimed in. There were murmurs of agreement as the Santas took their seats.

"Why didn't anyone like Harvey Nye?" Murphy asked.

"Ah, he was too full of himself." Number Five.

"He was a bully." Three.

"He made you feel like shit." Nine.

"Aw, Harvey wasn't that bad. A little big-headed is all." Six.

"Big-headed? The man was a fascist!" Ten.

"Just because he gave you a hard time—"

"I'm not the only one he gave a hard time! What are you, teacher's pet?"

Then everybody was shouting at once and Murphy had to yell for silence. *The Case of the Squabbling Santas*, he thought. "Okay, so Harvey was not a popular guy. But is that a reason to kill him? The training session is only three days long, for Pete's sake. There has to be some other motive."

"Not necessarily," said Santa Number Seven. "Harvey had the most aggravating personality of anyone I've ever met. I consider myself a mild-mannered, peace-loving man, but there were times when I would gladly have strangled the man myself. But I didn't," he added hastily.

"Truth is," Number Twelve added, "most of us felt that way, Lieutenant. Captain?"

"Sergeant," Murphy said. "I'm Sergeant Murphy, and for now I think we'll just stick with numbers for you." He let a silence develop as he looked over these living icons of goodwill toward all men and found what he was hunting for. "Number Eight!" Murphy barked. "Where's your beard?"

"I don't know," Number Eight said in a frightened young voice. "I got here late, while the others were on their break, and when I got changed I couldn't find the beard."

"How about that, Number Three?" Murphy asked, picking a number at random. "Was Number Eight late getting here?"

"Er, I didn't notice," Number Three said, startled at being singled out.

"I did," said Number Eleven, nodding vigorously and making the bell on his cap jingle. "He missed the first part of the session."

"Yeah, I saw him come in," Number Four confirmed. "He was late. He couldna done old Harve."

"I dunno," Santa Number One said with a surprisingly squeaky voice. "Harvey was always picking on Number Eight."

"Because Number Eight was always late!" snapped Number Thirteen.

"Now wait a minute!" Number Eight wailed.

"Let's all wait a minute," Murphy said. He wanted to know how long their break lasted. Fifteen minutes, they told him, from ten to ten-fifteen. Not really long enough for the killer to get out of his costume, put on Number Eight's, kill Harvey Nye, and change back into his own Santa suit before Number Eight showed up. "Number Eight, is your costume torn anywhere?"

The young Santa looked down at himself. "I don't think so."

"Then whose is? *Somebody's* suit is torn."

Silence for a moment. Then: "Mine is," Number Two said reluctantly. He lifted his beard to show a piece of red missing from the top of his suit. "It was all right when I took it off yesterday. And I might as well tell you—I couldn't find my beard either, so I took Number Eight's. But I didn't kill Harvey. I was with Number Seven and Number Thirteen all during the break."

"That's right," two voices spoke up.

"You took my beard?" Number Eight asked indignantly. Murphy waved him to silence. "Did you all go to the same place for your break?"

They didn't. Santas Number Two, Seven, and Thirteen were in the employees' cafeteria drinking coffee. Santas Number Five and Eleven went to the men's room. Numbers Three, Four, Ten, and Twelve spent their break in the Smoking Lounge. And Number Eight was late. That left Number One, Number Six, and Number Nine unaccounted for.

"I had to make a phone call," said Number One.

"I had to drop off a form at the Personnel Office," said Number Six.

"I got a Coke from the machine down the hall and stood there drinking it," said Number Nine.

Did anyone see them making the phone call, dropping off the form, drinking the Coke? No, three times. Murphy paused to think a moment. Harvey Nye had been alive and well before the break, busily instructing his students in the art of Santa-ing; the only difference from the day before was that today his class numbered twelve instead of the usual thirteen. Sometime during the break one of the Santas had slipped back into the classroom and strangled Harvey with the Christmas tree lights. And the killer had to be Number One, Number Six, or Number Nine—since the remaining ten alibied one another.

But before the session began, the killer had stolen Number Two's beard and ripped a piece from his costume in a clumsy attempt to incriminate the other Santa. Premeditation, no doubt about it. Sergeant Murphy asked, "Did any of you know Harvey Nye before this training session began?"

Haltingly, four hands went up into the air. The three suspects' . . . and Number Two's. "We've worked this gig before," Number Six explained. "The store makes us repeat the training session, though."

"That's okay," Number Nine said. "You forget the drill from one Christmas to the next. And we want to be the best Santa Clauses we can be, don't we?"

"Ha ha ha," said Number One mirthlessly.

Was it One, Six, or Nine? Murphy told them to stay . . . and Number Two as well. The other nine Santas could give their names and addresses to the police officers and then go.

"Hey, why am I staying?" Number Two protested. "I got two witnesses that say—"

"You were with them all during the break, I know," the police sergeant said as the other Santas got up and started filing out. "But the killer took your beard to plant as false evidence. I want to find out if he picked you at random or whether you were a deliberate choice."

The words "the killer" got through to them. Number Two stared at the other three Santas. "One of you guys is a, a *murderer!*" he blurted. It was just sinking in on the others as well. Numbers One, Six, and Nine eyed one another warily. They'd been so caught up in the not altogether unpleasurable notion that Harvey Nye was dead that they hadn't yet given much thought to how he got that way.

"Which one of you dropped off the form in the Personnel Office?" Murphy asked.

"Me," said Number Six.

"What's your name?"

"Jack Billings."

Murphy went to the door and motioned to one of the police officers.. "Go to the Personnel Office," he said. "Find out if a form was left there this morning by Jack Billings. If it was, see if you can pin down the time."

"Jack Billings," the officer repeated and left on his errand.

Murphy went back to Number Two and the three suspects. "So. You've all had this training session from Harvey before."

"Naw," squeaked Number One. "This was Harvey's first year as the instructor. Last year he was just a Santa like the rest of us."

Number Two nodded. "Me and Harvey and Will here— Number One—we been doin' this for six, seven years now."

"What about you two?" Murphy asked the others.

"This is my second year," Number Six said.

"My third," Number Nine added.

"Take off your beards," Murphy said abruptly. "Your hats, too . . . and wigs? Let me see what you look like."

The four near-identical Santa Clauses gradually metamorphosed into four individual men. Numbers One and Two were much older than the others, obviously retirees with time on their hands. Physically, they were of a type with Harvey Nye, evidently the build the store preferred in its Santas: burly, barrel-chested, big-shouldered, making Number One's squeaky voice all the more surprising. Number Two appeared to be the older of the two, with a full head of thick, wavy white hair. He was the only Santa who didn't have to wear a wig.

Number Six was in his forties, with a down-on-his-luck look about him. An enigma: Murphy couldn't get a fix on him. But it was Number Nine that surprised him. Like the tardy Number Eight, Number Nine was clearly a student. He was very young, and skinny to the point of emaciation. Murphy looked at the boy's thin wrists, thought of Harvey Nye's thick neck, and mentally dismissed Number Nine as a suspect.

He said, "What happened to the previous instructor?"

"Moved to Florida," Number One answered.

"And so Harvey was promoted. Why Harvey instead of one of you two?" Murphy meant the two older Santas.

"Because Harvey sabotaged us," Number Two said bluntly. "He went into Personnel and convinced them neither of us could do the job."

"He said nobody would listen to me," Number One squeaked. "Because of my voice. He said people laughed at me."

Number Two sighed. "He told them I was too old. Not enough stamina."

Professional jealousy among Santa Clauses? "And they believed him?"

"Personnel don't know squat," Number One said viciously. "Harvey wasn't even a good Santa Claus. He made the kids uncomfortable. He loved to lecture them—he was such a bully, he even bullied the little kids. Kids don't come to Santa Claus to be lectured. They want to talk about their wish lists, about what *they* are going to get out of Christmas this year. Some of the kids are unbelievable, and you want to squash 'em like the bedbugs they are. But even the good kids went away from Harvey on the verge of tears. But Harvey loved kids. Oh, yeah. He loved them because they couldn't fight back." Number One's squeak got higher. "You think Personnel noticed? You think they even had an *inkling* of what a bully Harvey Nye was? Ha! No, he smiled and turned on the charm and filled their ears with poison about me and George here, Number Two, I mean. He stole that job from me. From us. One of us shoulda got that promotion."

The other three Santas were listening to his tirade with fascination. "Who is Number One?" Six whispered to Two.

"You are Number Six," Number Two replied cryptically.

Just then a knock sounded at the door; it was the officer

Sergeant Murphy had sent to the Personnel Office. "Learn anything?" Murphy asked.

"Yeah. Woman in Personnel says Jack Billings dropped off his GSK-440D form this morning. She says she stepped out of her office at ten o'clock, and when she got back ten minutes later the form was on her desk."

Number Six whooped and threw his arms into the air. "Then I'm cleared?"

"You're cleared," Murphy agreed. "You can go. Leave your address and phone number with the officer."

Number Six, a.k.a. Jack Billings, jingled his way out of the room, not even glancing back at the two remaining suspects. Not his problem. The officer raised an eyebrow and closed the door.

So it was One or Nine. Murphy turned to Number Nine. "Strip."

"What?"

"I want you to strip down to your underwear. Go on. Do it."

Uncertainly, the boy started taking off his Santa costume, unwrapping what seemed like a ton of padding to reveal the full extent of his natural skinniness. When he was finished, he looked like a skeleton standing there in Jockey shorts and a T-shirt that said: *I think, therefore I is.*

Murphy stared straight into Number One's eye. "You know as well as I do that that kid could never have taken Harvey Nye in a struggle. Look at him, Number One! Harvey could have broken him in two like a stick. But you, on the other hand—you could have pulled that string of lights around Harvey's neck tight enough to get the job done. And, Number One . . . you're the only one left."

Number Two stared at his companion aghast. "Will?"

"You killed him," Murphy said flatly. "Nobody else had

means, motive, and opportunity. Number Nine there had opportunity but not the rest of it. You're it, Number One. Cooperate and things'll go easier for you."

The other man's eyes were watering as he turned away from Murphy to face Number Two. "That promotion shoulda gone to *me*, George!"

"Aw, Will!" George put his hand on Number One's shoulder.

Murphy noticed the gesture and said, "In case you've forgotten, Number Two, it was your beard and a piece of your costume that he left at the scene of the crime. You were his only remaining competition."

Slowly Number Two withdrew his hand.

"Wow," said Number Nine.

Murphy had almost forgotten him. "Get dressed, kid. Go on home. And don't forget to leave—"

"My name et cetera with the officer. Gotcha." Number Nine gathered up his Santa clothing and left.

The two old Santas sat staring at each other. "I'm sorry, George," Number One said. "I was just feeling so . . . so *cheated*, ya know?"

"So you decided to put the blame on me?" Number Two stood up and shook his head. "I'm sorry too, Will. I'm sorry you thought you had to do this. You deserve whatever you get." Still shaking his head, he trudged heavily out of the room, not a happy Santa.

Number One didn't even seem to hear his rights being read to him. "That promotion shoulda gone to me!" he insisted stubbornly. "I was a better Santa Claus!"

"Ho ho ho," said Sergeant Murphy.

I felt this collection would be lacking if I failed to include one "cross-over" story—a story that's both mystery and science fiction. All science fiction stories are mysteries anyway, in the sense that they concern something out of the ordinary that needs to be puzzled out. A problem in search of a solution. Perhaps that's true of all fiction—which could explain the enduring nature of the mystery genre; it deals with pretty basic stuff. In "Play Nice" the two genres combine to illustrate one universal truth that can never be repeated too often: Always listen to Mother.

PLAY NICE

The three of them sat fidgeting, waiting for Mother to tell them they could go. Duncan could hear Hartley muttering to himself; not a peep out of Britt, although she was eager to get going. But until Mother gave them the green light, all they could do was sit and wait. And she was taking her time about it. It seemed the older she got, the more cautious she became.

"What's taking her so long?" Hartley grumbled.

Duncan sighed. Hartley had this need to vocalize, to say out loud what everyone else was thinking. Once he got started, he'd go on and on until Britt lost her patience—which she was doing a lot lately—and told him to shut up.

"What's she waiting for?" Hartley complained. "Fuss, fuss, fuss. What's the hold-up? Dammit, she's getting obsessive, scared to let us out of her sight. Hoo, will I be glad to get out of here! Duncan, talk to her. Tell her we're ready to go."

Duncan didn't bother to answer. They'd go when Mother said go.

"You know what I think?" Hartley went on. "I think she just likes to make us wait. Demonstration of power, like that. You think she's possessive now? The day's coming when she won't allow us any independent movement at all, you wait and see. Yeah. We'll just be puppets, all three of us, doing what Mother says do, going where Mother says go *when* she says go—"

"Shut up, Hartley!" Britt snapped.

It was another five minutes before Mother spoke to them. "You may go now," she said softly. "Be careful."

Duncan gave a silent cheer. They'd been cooped up too long; everyone was getting edgy. Mother did take good care of them, but sometimes . . .

His instrument panel gave him the *Clear* signal; he checked the feed from Britt and Hartley and flipped the switch that completed the disengage sequence. The hatches opened, the anchor grapples uncoupled, and the three single-occupancy shuttles dropped away from the mothership, arcing gracefully into a tight orbit around the strange planet below. See you later, Ma.

"Strange" planet only because unfamiliar; and unfamiliar only to them. The colony world of Pirmacha was prosperous and self-sufficient, able up to now to handle its own problems. But this time the Pirmachans had put in a request to Central for outside help; Duncan and his team got the nod. Duncan had no worries about Britt, but he wasn't certain Hartley would settle down in time to get the job done; Hartley rather envisioned himself as a Young Turk when in fact he was merely young.

The shuttles automatically locked in on Pirmacha's homing beacon and let themselves be guided to the colony's landing field. Mother's voice spoke in their ears. "Force wall is up. The Pirmachans wish you to undergo decontamination."

Hartley said something obscene.

"It's an obvious requirement, Hartley," Mother said in a tone of mild reprimand. "You know that. They may have requested your help, but you are a guest on their world and you will behave like one."

"Yes, Mother," Hartley said with all the sarcasm at his command. Britt snickered. "I swear to God," Hartley growled as he climbed out of his shuttle, "on the next circuit, I'm going on a nonsentient ship or I'm not going."

"You don't mean that," Britt said sharply. "Putting your life in the hands of strangers? Relying on quick responses on the part of crew members you don't even know?"

"Yeah, tell me about it," Hartley grumbled.

"I'm trying to," Britt replied earnestly. "You've never traveled on a nonsentient ship, Hartley—I have. Even a 619-X ship computer can't handle every emergency without a human initiator. What if somebody forgets to start some necessary repair sequencing? Or is two seconds too slow? You could *die*, Hartley."

"Uh—"

"So the artificial intelligences in the motherships take their 'protector' function a little too seriously—so what? You put up with it."

Hartley was silent a moment, and then said, "You're quite right, Britt. I fell into the trap of taking Mother for granted. It's a mistake I'll not make again." His voice was low and somber.

Duncan swallowed a laugh. He'd seen it before: the

minute Hartley got out of physical contact with the mothership, he became more lordly and magisterial. Not that any of them ever truly got away from Mother, thanks to their implanted communicators. She'd been listening to every word.

No Pirmachans were in sight. The three visitors followed flashing green arrows to a small building apart from the regular landing field facilities. Inside, the automatics put them through the standard decontamination procedures, a process that required only twenty minutes.

"The force wall is down," Mother's voice spoke in their ears. "A Pirmachan is waiting for you by Exit One."

Outside the exit, a woman with close-cropped gray hair and angry brown eyes stood glaring at them. "You certainly took your time getting here," she said abruptly. "Which is the Prime Arbiter?"

Duncan raised an eyebrow. "I am." He gestured toward Britt. "Second Arbiter." Then Hartley. "Third Arbiter." They never identified themselves by name when called upon to sit in judgment.

The Pirmachan woman nodded briefly. "My name is Copely. I've been delegated by the High Council to be your escort while you are on Pirmacha. This way." No time wasted on amenities; just let's-get-on-with-it.

Copely led the three Circuit Arbiters to ground transport nearby. Their route to the city led them past one of the planet's famous horsebreeding facilities, with its bioclean stables and sweeping exercise grounds. Although the breeding and training of racehorses had been only a minor enterprise when the colony was first established, Pirmacha had eventually found itself galaxy-famous as one of the few places left where the purebred Arabian could still be found. Other earth strains had been hopelessly interbred with the multiplicity of equine species encountered in other star systems, from the dragon-sized *Donnerpferde* on Wagner's World to those eight-legged oddities in the Aldebaran IV system.

But Pirmacha had no indigenous horses, and the colonists had wisely forbidden the importation of any horses at all once their Arabian stock was established and flourishing. And that decision had made their fortune. An ugly disease called osteodisjunctus, picked up on some outlying world and spread from planet to planet, was able to lie dormant for four or five generations before bursting forth to wipe out horses by the herd. There was no cure, not even a treatment; the disease struck swiftly and inexorably. But no case of osteodisjunctus had ever been reported among Pirmachan Arabians, however; and horsebreeders everywhere began turning to Pirmacha for "clean" stock with which to rebuild their stables.

On the other side of a faintly shimmering force wall, a handsome colt with more energy than he knew what to do with easily paced their ground transport. The three newcomers to Pirmacha admired the small head, the graceful sweep of the neck, the seemingly effortless movement of the slender legs. Then suddenly the colt tired of the game and bolted away. It was a safe guess that the reason the tribunal had been summoned to Pirmacha had something to do with the horses. The Pirmachan High Council had been stingy with details in their request for aid. They'd said only that a murder had been committed; and that while Security had narrowed the number of suspects to two, High Council had been unable to determine which of the two was guilty. The Pirmachan request for an outside tribunal had concluded with the assertion that the case was dividing the Pirmachan people and an early resolution was imperative.

"The schism," Mother prompted.

Right. "Copely," Duncan said as they approached the city, "exactly how is this murder case dividing the people? Is everyone taking sides, or what?"

Copely snorted. "You could say that. The two suspects are named Roj Kordan and Anita Verdoris. Does that mean anything to you?"

"Owners?" Britt guessed.

"Owners of the two biggest spreads on Pirmacha," Copely confirmed. "That's Kordan's land you're looking at now. Every small breeder here is dependent in some way on either Kordan or Verdoris—for off-planet animal transport, specialized veterinary medicine, stud service, you name it. Every single person here with any connection to horses whatsoever has a stake in the outcome."

"And that's why you asked for us," Duncan said suddenly. "Whichever way High Council decided, they'd alienate half the population. You're passing the buck."

"Duncan!" Mother's voice said sharply in his ear. "That's not the *kind* of judgement you've been called on to render here. Apologize to her. Quickly."

Damn; she was right. "Copely, I'm sorry—that was out of line," Duncan said hurriedly. "Of course you want outside judges. You're all too close to the matter to be impartial, and you have the good sense to know it."

The Pirmachan woman grunted something unintelligible.

"Really, Duncan," Mother murmured in his ear. "You're the senior member of this tribunal. You're supposed to know better."

Duncan touched the spot behind his right ear where the communicator was implanted and wished, not for the first time, that the thing came with an on/off switch. He exchanged glances with Britt and Hartley. So they'd been handed a political hot potato; it wouldn't be the first time.

They'd left the open horse country and entered the city. Hartley coughed politely and asked, "What was the victim's name?"

"Longstride," Copely told him. "He was found in the Kordan stables with his throat cut. You'll find all the details in your console brief."

No attempt to make it look like an accident, then. They came to the High Council Building without further talk. It was there they would hear testimony via remote visuals and ultimately render their verdict.

The hallways were crowded with visitors who'd come to gawk at the three Arbiters. They all had that same angry look that Copely had, some of them even seething; the place seemed ready to explode. "Best wrap this up fast," Duncan said in a low voice to the other two as they entered the Judgement Chamber.

Copely activated their consoles for them and retired to a corner, making herself available if needed while the three Arbiters studied the brief the High Council had prepared for them. Regardless of all that might be going on in the background, the facts of the crime were fairly simple.

At dawn eight days earlier, a stablehand at Roj Kordan's main facility had been getting ready for the day's work when he'd caught a whiff of the sickly sweet smell of blood. He'd followed the scent to an unused stall, where he'd found Longstride lying on the floor and bleeding profusely from the deep gash in his throat. By the time the stablehand was able to summon help, Longstride had died; the stablehand must have missed the murderer by only minutes. Suspicion immediately fell upon Verdoris, the woman who was Kordan's only real rival on Pirmacha.

"Who was this Longstride?" Hartley asked. "Did he work there?"

But Britt had guessed it. "Longstride was a horse," she said disgustedly. They'd been brought across four star systems to determine who had killed a *horse*.

"Not just *a* horse," Copely spoke up from the corner. "He was the premiere stud on Pirmacha. His get has the best win record in the galaxy, bar none. Kordan had a seven-year waiting list for Longstride."

Hartley stood up. "I don't care if he had a *seventy*-year waiting list. You brought us here through false petition of duress—do you know the penalty for that?"

"There was nothing false about it!" Copely protested. "Longstride's murder has generated violence here—Kordan's people and Verdoris's have already come to blows on a number of occasions. Someone's going to get killed if this isn't settled soon. We may even have civil war!"

"Over a horse?" Duncan asked mildly.

"Not just *a* horse!" Copely was practically screaming at them. "How can you render a just verdict when you don't even try to understand?"

"We don't intend to," Hartley said angrily. "At least, I don't. I refuse to hear the case."

"Hartley!" Mother said sharply. "Remember why you're there!"

"Keep out of this, Mother," Duncan commanded. "This is our bailiwick."

"What?" Copely said, confused.

"Talking to the ship," Britt explained.

Hartley whirled around. "I'm leaving," he announced.

"You'll do no such thing," Mother huffed, ignoring Duncan's instructions to mind her own business. "You're on duty—get back there!"

"I'm going on private time as of now."

"You have no private time coming."

"Then take it out of next week's allowance!" Hartley snarled, and slammed out of the room.

The Third Arbiter calmed down quickly enough, once Duncan and Britt followed him out of the High Council Building. They looked for, and found, a quiet watering place where they could talk. Copely trailed in after them, their angry shadow, and took a seat where she could keep an eye on them.

"You aren't seriously thinking of hearing this case, are you?" Hartley asked Duncan once their drinks had been served.

"I think we'd better find out more of what's going on here. Mother? Are you there?"

"Of course, Duncan."

"Can you access the Pirmachan newsnets? Give us a run-down on just how serious a schism has developed here?"

"One moment."

Britt took a sip of her drink and said, "That should have been included in our briefing."

"A lot of things should have been included in our briefing," Duncan agreed. "But it's clear why the Pirmachans held back. Central would never have sent an arbitration team if they'd known the murder victim was a horse."

"Not just *a* horse," Britt said wryly, mimicking Copely.

Hartley shot a glance at the Councilwoman, who was nursing a drink and glaring at them angrily. "She has a lot of hostility, that one."

"Personal involvement, you think?" Duncan asked. "More than she's told us?"

Hartley just shrugged.

Mother had completed her scan of the local newsnets. "Evidently the schism is more serious than we thought." Duncan winced at the *we*. "Not only have there been outbreaks of violence," Mother went on, "but normal business operations have been interrupted to a dangerous extent. I'll give you an example. Off-planet animal transport is handled by a monopoly whose employees all have ties to either Kordan or Verdoris. A docking chief has a brother who supplies feed to Verdoris, a safety inspector moonlights as a scout for Kordan, and so on. When Kordan wanted to ship a consignment of Arabian brood mares to Burleigh's Planet, all the Verdoris-supporters refused to handle the shipment. The mares are still here, unpaid for. That sort of divisiveness has affected every aspect of Pirmachan life—food, machinery, simple maintenance."

"*Every* aspect?" Britt asked dubiously.

"Just about," Mother replied. "Like the Pirmachan Research Institute. Kordan commissioned them to do some specialized research in horse DNA. But a Verdoris-supporter managed to sabotage the Institute's back-up generator and then cut off the power supply for an hour, until Security broke into the control room and arrested him. But an hour was long enough for the experiments to be ruined—at enormous cost to the Institute, which of course was not paid by Kordan."

"So you're saying Pirmacha's economy is in danger?" Duncan asked.

"Most assuredly."

Hartley snorted. "And all because of a horse named Longstride!"

"Longstride is the excuse, Hartley," Mother said mildly. "This economic war between Kordan and Verdoris has been building up for a long time."

The three Arbiters were silent for a moment. Then Duncan said, "We're going to have to hear the case. There's too much at stake not to."

The other two reluctantly agreed. Then Britt squinted her eyes and announced, "I think we have company."

A stocky man in his middle years stood talking to Copely, both of them eyeing the three Arbiters. Then the man nodded and headed their way, broadcasting animosity as he came. "What's this I've been told?" he demanded in a bellicose voice. "You're not even going to hear the case?"

"On the contrary, sir, we have every intention of hearing the case," Duncan replied with exaggerated courtesy. "And you are . . . ?"

Taken aback, the man pulled out a bright green kerchief and mopped his balding forehead. "Forgive me, Arbiters. You are our last chance to resolve our . . . difficulties. My name is Thorin Glimm." He sat down at their table uninvited and said, "I'm Roj Kordan's Chief of Veterinary Services. I can't get the medicines I need or even ordinary lab supplies. Shipping is crippled here, virtually nonexistent—Verdoris's people have seen to that. And with Kordan locked in Security Isolation, nobody's making the decisions that have to be made."

"But surely Verdoris has need of shipping, too," Britt pointed out. "It can't be all her fault, Dr. Glimm. If you're aligned with Kordan—"

Glimm laughed shortly. "Arbiter, I am probably the only man on Pirmacha with a foot in both camps. I work for Kordan, but my daughter is married to Verdoris's eldest son. I'm going to get hurt whichever way you decide." He sighed. "I don't want either my employer or my son-in-law's mother to be blamed. But *one* of them is responsible for killing Longstride . . . or having him killed, more likely. And the only way to get this place back on track is to settle for once and for all the question of *which* one."

Hartley opened his mouth to speak, but Duncan shot him a warning look. They'd all been wondering why Kordan had been accused, why he would want to kill his own superhorse. But Duncan didn't want Hartley asking about it; all that information would be in the depositions and the testimony. Even this much outside chat was not good. "Doctor, I must ask you not to discuss the facts of the case."

"Of course, of course." Glimm marshaled his thoughts. "I'm just trying to impress upon you the importance of reaching a decisive conclusion. 'Not proved' or one of those other vague and unhelpful verdicts simply won't do. People have to *know* who killed Longstride, they have to be sure in their own minds that the killer didn't get away with it. It must be settled."

"That's what we're here for," Hartley said blandly.

Glimm looked at each of them in turn. "If you can't decide which is guilty . . ." He hesitated.

"If we can't?" Duncan prompted.

The veterinarian patted his forehead with the green kerchief again. "Then flip a coin. But come up with a name. *Settle this.*"

Without another word he pushed away from the table and lumbered out of the room, watched by Copely as well as by the three Arbiters. "The man must be torn," Britt said sympathetically. "He lives his life inside the Kordan camp. Yet anything that hurts Verdoris, hurts his daughter. But still he comes here and tells us to chance condemning an innocent person rather than reach no decision."

"How tough can it be?" Hartley wanted to know. "Reaching a decision. We can demand further investigations if we spot something they overlooked."

"We may have to do that," Duncan agreed. "We'll need to go over Security's evidence *very* carefully."

"Then you'd better get cracking," said Mother.

In so horse-conscious an environment, Pirmachan law was, quite naturally, severe on those who brought harm to another person's stock in any way whatsoever. The penalty for the destruction or even incapacitating of a horse was extreme: permanent exile from Pirmacha, with all the goods and property of the offender forfeit to the owner of the horse in question. So if Verdoris was guilty of killing Longstride, then Kordan would end up with a virtual monopoly and thus become the most powerful figure on Pirmacha. And vice versa.

"No wonder they're all up in arms," Britt said. "For them, it's a matter of which one of the two accused is going to end up running the planet. Hell of a way to hold an election." Duncan turned to Copely, sitting quietly in her corner of the Judgement Chamber. "Has this penalty ever been invoked before?"

"In the early years of colonization, frequently," Copely said. "But in my lifetime, only once. Verdoris was the injured party in that case. A rival breeder hamstrung a promising colt Verdoris had just entered in his maiden race. Verdoris collected enough from that judgement to let her challenge Kordan for dominance of the business."

"So Verdoris is familiar with the procedure," Hartley remarked. "That's interesting."

"Is it." Not a question. Copely was a Verdoris-supporter?

They began hearing testimony via remote, the holographic images of the witnesses appearing in the Judgement Chamber. They heard the stablehand testify how he'd found

Longstride bleeding to death. They heard from one of Kordan's trainers, whom the stablehand had gone running to for help. They listened to various Security Officers explain how a dropped electronic lockpick had led them to take Verdoris into custody: her fingerprints were all over the gadget.

Then they heard the witness who at last made it clear why Kordan had also been taken into custody, a suspect in the slaughter of his own prize money-making stallion. The witness who explained it all was none other than Thorin Glimm, Kordan's Chief of Veterinary Services.

Glimm was a reluctant witness, testifying only after being informed by Pirmachan Security that they'd get permission to use a hypnotic drug on him if necessary. The veterinarian's hologram showed a troubled face and the body language of discouragement. "Longstride was finished," he said unhappily. "He suffered a viral infection last winter, and ever since then his sperm count has been way down. We tried every treatment known, but Longstride responded to none of them. We even had the Research Institute working on his DNA, until that fool working for Verdoris cut off the power and destroyed the cultures. Those experiments were our only hope."

Duncan asked, "Couldn't new experiments have been conducted?"

"Yes, Kordan was scheduled to take new blood and tissue samples to the Institute the very day Longstride was murdered. Now, of course, it no longer matters."

Mother spoke. "Ask who was conducting the experiments."

Duncan cut off the sound to Glimm. "Mother, I've told you before—don't meddle. We'll call you when we need you."

"But you ought to know who—"

"And we'll get to it. Now butt out."

Mother sniffed.

"Jeez," said Hartley, shaking his head.

"Forget Mother," Britt said curtly. "Now we have a motive for Kordan. Longstride was no longer a valuable animal. If Kordan could kill him and shift the blame to Verdoris, he'd put her out of business."

"Only if Verdoris didn't know about Longstride." Duncan turned the sound back on. "Dr. Glimm, who else knew Longstride's sperm count was down?"

"Kordan and I were the only ones. I did the lab work myself. Kordan ordered me not to say anything." Glimm was looking more and more unhappy.

So Verdoris did *not* know Longstride's earning capacity was no longer a threat to her own stables. The three Arbiters mulled that over, and then Hartley said, "I think it's time we heard from the two suspects."

They called Verdoris first. She was a big woman, large-boned and strong looking. She held her head high as her hologram stared straight at them. "I wish to make a statement," she announced in a tight voice.

Not an unusual request. "Proceed," said Duncan.

"I did not kill Longstride," the big woman said. "I do not know who did. I did not order, hire, or even hint to those around me that I wanted Longstride dead. The electronic lockpick must be mine, since my fingerprints are on it. But I have no idea how it got into Kordan's stable. *I* did not leave it there."

"What were you doing with a lockpick in the first place?" Britt asked.

"We all use them," Verdoris said. "Everyone who breeds horses keeps a set of picks. They're handy when you need a

167

quick bypass of your internal security system."

"But this pick was keyed to Kordan's security system."

Verdoris spread her hands. "That, I have no explanation for. It would seem to indicate that one of my employees simply picked it up and used it. But for it to work on Kordan's system, someone inside Kordan's organization had to have provided him with the keycodes."

"Conspiracy?"

"It's the only explanation I can think of."

"To what benefit? How would one of your employees and one of Kordan's profit from the death of Longstride?"

"I don't know, Arbiter. I *sincerely* hope you will find out."

They questioned her further but learned nothing germane. Verdoris said she was with her husband at the time Longstride was killed, but she could easily have hired someone to do the deed in spite of her protestations to the contrary. Finally Duncan dismissed her and called Roj Kordan to testify.

Kordan was a dark, bearded man whose image blinked into existence breathing fire. "What have you found out about who killed my horse?" he demanded. When Duncan reminded him that he was one of the suspects, Kordan snorted. "I hadn't given up on Longstride yet. There were lab tests yet to be run, DNA tests. You don't understand about Longstride. Even if I were convinced his stud days were over—which I wasn't—I wouldn't have had him killed. Never. Not Longstride."

Hartley asked, "Why did you order Dr. Glimm not to tell anyone about the horse's low sperm count?"

Another snort. "Is that a serious question? Longstride was a goldmine, Arbiter. I didn't want any rumors circulating until I was sure beyond all doubt that he'd sired his last foal. And I was still a long way from being sure."

"Who do you think killed Longstride?"

"It had to be Anita Verdoris. Her prints were on the pick."

"Couldn't the pick have been stolen by someone in her employ?"

"Only if she was careless enough to leave it lying around. And Verdoris is not careless."

Duncan spoke up. "Do you mean to say no one could steal one of *your* electronic picks if he set his mind to it?"

"Not very likely."

"But possible."

Kordan glowered. "Yes."

"And where were you when Longstride was killed?"

"At Exercise Yard B—there's a filly I wanted to watch work out. Other people saw me there, plenty of them."

Same as with Verdoris, then; Kordan could have sent someone else to do the killing while establishing an alibi for himself elsewhere. Duncan let the irate owner go and called the head of the Research Institute.

She had little to tell them. Kordan had asked the Institute for a complete work-up of Longstride's DNA. They'd barely prepared the first batch of cultures when Verdoris's man cut the power and ruined all their samples. The experiments proper hadn't even been started.

Duncan dismissed her and sat staring glumly at Copely in her corner; the Councilwoman's face was impassive. They had no grounds for eliminating either Kordan or Verdoris as a suspect. Nor did they have grounds for convicting either of them. No wonder the Pirmachan High Council had asked for help.

Hartley said, "We'll have to use B-Aminosine. That's the only way we're going to find out who's telling the truth."

"We can't use it," Britt objected. "It's too dangerous."

"It's the only hypnotic drug that's one hundred percent reliable."

"That doesn't matter, Hartley. B-Aminosine-induced testimony has been ruled inadmissible. We can't use it."

"Wait a minute," Duncan said. "I'm not sure we've got a ruling from Central on that yet. Mother—check on the status of the hypnotics exclusion law, please. See if it's still in Current Dockets." Silence. "Mother? Respond, please."

Her voice, when she spoke, seemed to have lost its usual gentleness. "Are you sure I won't be *butting in?*"

Duncan ignored the sarcasm and repeated his request. Mother, still miffed, reported that a ruling excluding the use of B-Aminosine was expected momentarily but was not yet on the books.

"Then we can get in under the wire," Hartley said. "Britt?" She nodded. "Duncan?"

"Let's do it," Duncan said. "And this time not by remote. Copely," he called, "I want Anita Verdoris and Roj Kordan right here in this chamber."

Anyone injected with B-Aminosine could count on being sick as a dog for anywhere from three days to two weeks: nausea, dizziness, headaches, cold sweats, blurred vision, loss of motor functions. Several cases of partial paralysis of the central nervous system had been reported, and at least one death had been directly attributed to the administration of B-Aminosine. Only an Arbiter could order the use of the drug.

The Arbiters' decision to subject the two prime suspects to the possibly detrimental effects of B-Aminosine was met with more relief than apprehension by the Pirmachans who heard about it. Suffering a little temporary illness, no matter how unpleasant, was a small price to pay to get at the truth—especially since it was someone else who'd be doing the suffering. The doctor called in to administer the drug had insisted an adjoining chamber be turned into a recovery room before he would proceed; finally he and his team were ready.

Roj Kordan was first. As soon as he went under, the doctor stepped back to allow the Arbiters to question him.

Duncan wasted no time. "Kordan, can you hear me?"

"Yes."

"Did you kill Longstride?"

"No."

"Did you arrange to have him killed?"

"No."

"Do you know who did kill him?"

"No."

Duncan nodded. "That's all we need to know," he said to the doctor. "Bring him out of it."

Kordan came back to consciousness retching and shaking. Unable to walk, he was carried by the doctor's assistants to the recovery room.

The Arbiters tried not to give anything away through their facial expressions as their one remaining suspect was brought in. But Anita Verdoris glanced at Copely and read the truth there. "He passed the test, didn't he?" she asked.

Copely looked away.

Whatever hope the Arbiters entertained that they had identified Longstride's killer was quickly quashed. Verdoris's B-Aminosine session went exactly the way Kordan's had gone. Did you kill, did you arrange, do you know. *No. No. No.* The three Arbiters looked at one another despairingly as Verdoris was carried out.

Mother broke her long silence. "*Now* what are you going to do, Mr. Know-It-All?"

171

★ ★ ★ ★ ★

What they did was take a break.

Copely led them to private lodgings, saw they were served a meal, and left them alone. By mutual unspoken agreement, no one mentioned the case they were to decide until they'd finished eating and were indulging in an after-dinner drink.

Duncan took the lead. "It hasn't all been wasted effort," he said. "We did succeed in establishing the innocence of both Verdoris and Kordan. Now we know to look elsewhere."

"Where do we start?" Britt asked.

Hartley scowled. "Did somebody say we ought to wrap this one up fast? Hah. We're going to have to start over, right from the beginning. Anyone on this horsey planet could have done it."

"Anyone except Verdoris and Kordan," Britt said absently.

"We could be here for months! And all because some ex-stud of a racehorse was made into a symbol of the power struggle going on between those two." Hartley's voice was rising. "So what do we do, question the entire population?"

"Take it easy, Hartley," Duncan said. "We won't have to go that far."

"Why not?" Hartley asked loudly. "Line 'em up, shoot 'em full of B-Aminosine, and ask 'em one question. Did you do it? Sooner or later somebody will say *yes*."

Duncan laughed uncomfortably. "And leave behind us an entire planet full of people too sick to take care of themselves?"

Hartley got up from the table and crossed over to look out a window. "Serve them right," he muttered. "This is a ridiculous situation they've put us in."

Britt sat motionless, watching the two men.

Duncan rose slowly. "Hartley? You're not serious?"

"I'm not?" the other man answered enigmatically.

"You can't be! The entire population . . . for one thing, the local supply of B-Aminosine—"

"—will be adequate for our purposes," Hartley finished for him. "You know damned well the guilty person is someone close to either Kordan or Verdoris. We start with them."

Duncan stared at him unbelieving. Then he appealed to Britt. "Britt, help me out here!"

She licked her lips, taking her time. "You know, Duncan . . . he may be right."

"Britt!"

"All we'd have to do is *announce* we're testing everybody," she said carefully. "And then start testing, to prove it. Whoever's guilty will most likely come forward and admit it. He'll know he's going to be caught anyway—why put himself through the agony of a B-Aminosine illness?"

"And if he doesn't come forward?"

"Then we do test everybody," Hartley said harshly. "We requisition more of the drug from Central if we have to."

Duncan hesitated. "It would work," Britt said. "Do you know any other way to flush out the killer, Duncan? I'll listen, if you do."

Hartley muttered, "There is no other way."

Duncan was still not convinced. "But to drug-test an entire population—there's no precedent for that in the entire history of Arbitration! And it's still a dangerous drug!"

Britt smiled wryly. "You didn't seem too worried about that when we tested Verdoris and Kordan."

The First Arbiter was silent. Then: "I'll agree to the *announcement* of planetwide testing. But if early testing doesn't turn up Longstride's killer—"

"Why don't we put off deciding about that until the time comes?" Britt interrupted. "First things first."

"How about it, Duncan?" Hartley asked. "Are we agreed?"

Duncan pressed his lips together. "Agreed."

"ARE YOU OUT OF YOUR PEA-PICKIN' MINDS?" Mother roared.

All three Arbiters winced. "What's wrong?" Duncan asked.

"You are actually going to use that *nasty* drug on innocent people—because you're too unobservant to see what's staring you right in the face?"

"Now, wait a minute," Hartley said angrily.

"I have never seen such sloppy work in my life," Mother went on indignantly. "Sloppy, sloppy, sloppy! How many times have I told you that if a thing is worth doing at all, it's worth doing well?"

About thirty thousand, Duncan guessed.

Mother switched her mode of speaking; now she spoke slow-ly and care-ful-ly, so the dumbbunnies she was talking to could understand. "You don't have to drug the entire populace. The answer is right there under your nose. Remember the man who cut the power at the Research Institute? Verdoris's employee? The one who caused Longstride's DNA cultures to be ruined. Remember him? Think hard, now."

Duncan clenched his teeth. "What about him?"

"You never questioned him."

Britt looked puzzled. "Is there some reason we should have? That was just one of several violent incidents that erupted after Longstride was killed."

"Was it, now. Try thinking in sequence for a change.

What was Kordan planning to do on the day Longstride died?"

Duncan slapped his forehead. "He was planning to take new tissue samples in for testing! The power disruption at the Institute came *before* the horse was killed!"

"And you never even noticed that," Mother said reprovingly. "As I said, sloppy. All right, then. First Longstride's DNA is destroyed. Then Longstride himself is destroyed. Does that suggest anything to you?"

The three Arbiters exchanged blank looks. Then Britt said: "Someone was trying to remove all traces of Longstride?"

A biomechanical sigh. "Now you're on the right track. By the way, you didn't tell me to access financial records, but I did it anyway." Mother paused for effect. "The fellow who cut the power at the Institute was paid to do it. A nice sum was transferred to his account the day after the incident, and I traced the source of the transfer. I know who paid him."

The three Arbiters waited expectantly. *She just has to make us ask,* Duncan thought. "Who, Mother?"

Mother took her time, milking it. "Dr. Glimm."

"The vet?" Britt said. "But why would he . . . ?"

"Why don't you ask him?" Mother said sweetly. "You can always threaten him with B-Aminosine."

"We can always *use* B-Aminosine," Hartley growled.

"That won't be necessary," Mother informed them. "The man knows drugs. Just let him see what you have in mind and he'll talk. There's one other thing—Longstride's low sperm count. How many people knew about it?"

"Two," said Hartley. "Kordan and Dr. Glimm."

"Exactly. And Security supposedly had to use the threat of drug-testing to get Dr. Glimm to testify about it. So how did Security know to question him in the first place?"

"Ahhhh," Hartley said. "He had to have leaked it. Kordan sure as hell wouldn't have said anything. But why would Glimm want Longstride's condition known?"

"As a cover story," Duncan said suddenly. "Something else was wrong with Longstride—something so wrong that Dr. Glimm couldn't even tell the horse's owner about it. So wrong that the horse had to be destroyed."

"At last!" Mother said with approval. "I was beginning to think you'd never get there. Well? What are you standing around here for? Get hopping!"

"Yes, Mother," three voices said.

Mother was right. As soon as Dr. Glimm saw the medical team waiting in the Judgement Chamber, all the life drained out of him. He was caught and he knew it. Glimm shook his head when Duncan asked if they'd need the drug. The medical team quietly departed, leaving only Copely behind to listen with the Arbiters.

"It was osteodisjunctus." Dr. Glimm slumped down in a chair and stared at his feet. "Do you know what that is? It's a horse-killer, the worst disease a horse can get. Absolutely virulent, absolutely unstoppable."

"Longstride had osteodisjunctus?" Duncan asked.

"He was a carrier. I spotted an anomaly in his blood two years ago," the veterinarian said. "But I didn't know what it was—it didn't match the known structure of the disease's causative organism. It took me two years of off-and-on testing to identify it as a mutated form. And all that time Longstride's infected sperm was being shipped all over the galaxy. If it ever got out that I had known for two years . . ." He shook his head sadly, leaving the thought unfinished.

So, he was protecting himself, Duncan thought. Not

Kordan, not Pirmacha's reputation as a reliable source of disease-free horses. Himself. "There was nothing wrong with Longstride's sperm count, was there?"

"Hell, no, it was as high as ever. He had years of stud service left in him. But I had to think of something to make Kordan stop breeding him."

Mother spoke to the three Arbiters. "You should have asked to see the sperm-count test results," she said reprovingly. None of them answered her; just one more place they'd slipped up.

Britt had a question for the veterinarian. "How did you get hold of Verdoris's electronic lockpick?"

"From my daughter's home," Glimm said. "I mentioned that she's married to Verdoris's son, didn't I? I was visiting one day when he came in carrying his mother's lockpick—something was wrong with his own and he'd borrowed hers. He happened to be wearing gloves and the thought occurred to me that her fingerprints must be on the pick. I simply took it when no one was looking."

"And left it at the scene to incriminate Verdoris. Is that the same reason you bribed one of her employees to cut the power at the Research Institute?"

"Yes." Miserably.

Duncan said, "Dr. Glimm, why so brutal a method of killing the horse? Surely a lethal injection would have been more humane."

Glimm gave a humorless laugh. "And who would have been the first one to be suspected? No, I had to do it in a way to direct suspicion away from myself." He was silent a moment, and then added: "Arbiters, you never knew Longstride. He was a magnificent animal, truly magnificent. Killing him was the worst thing I've ever had to do in my life. I felt as if I were cutting my own throat."

And so you were. Duncan glanced at the other two Arbiters. Britt and Hartley shook their heads; no more questions. It was time to pronounce judgement.

"Dr. Thorin Glimm," Duncan said, "you are hereby sentenced to exile from Pirmacha for the rest of your natural life. If you ever attempt to return to Pirmacha for any reason whatsoever, you will be incarcerated for a period of time to be determined by a later tribunal. Moreover, all your goods and property are forfeit to Roj Kordan in partial recompense for the grievous harm you have done him. Do you understand the sentence?"

"I do, yes."

Duncan's tone softened. "Dr. Glimm, you'll be given time to settle your affairs before your exile begins. But you do understand, don't you, that you'll not be allowed to practice veterinary medicine ever again?"

Glimm nodded. "It doesn't matter. Somehow . . . somehow I just don't have the heart for it anymore."

At Duncan's signal, Copely summoned the Security Officers to take Glimm away. His head sagged down on his chest as he left, suddenly an old man.

"Thank God that's over," Hartley said with a sigh of relief. "Now we can get out of here."

But Mother had to have the last word. "At least you cleaned up after yourselves," she admitted grudgingly. "But don't you ever, *ever* make such a mess again!"

Copely was driving them back to the landing field where their shuttles waited. The Councilwoman was all smiles, a startling contrast to her dour anger on the trip in. "The only downside is that Glimm's daughter will lose her inheritance," she was saying. "Sins of the fathers. But she's hardly left out in the cold. She's part of the Verdoris family now."

"It's *your* law," Hartley said shortly.

"Oh, I wasn't criticizing," Copely said with a smile. "In fact, we're eternally grateful to you. You not only found Longstride's killer, you also alerted us to a greater danger."

"You mean the osteodisjunctus," Duncan said.

"That's what I mean. We'll shut down operations for a while, until we can do a thorough testing of all the livestock on Pirmacha. If we find any examples of Dr. Glimm's 'anomaly' in the blood . . ."

"What will you do?" Britt asked.

"Destroy the carriers, of course," Copely said. "But in a more humane manner than the way Dr. Glimm dispatched poor Longstride." She sighed. "I wish you could have met Longstride, Arbiters. He was the greatest horse I have ever known."

Duncan half expected a sarcastic comment from Mother, but none came.

They reached the landing field. With repeated expressions of gratitude, Copely bade them farewell. The Arbiters had been on Pirmacha less than a full realtime day, but to Duncan it seemed like a year. Britt and Hartley looked every bit as drained as he felt, pinch-faced and not at all pleased with themselves. Today had not been the team's most stellar performance; none of the three would ever be regaling grandchildren with stories of Pirmacha.

Wearily Duncan climbed into his shuttle, wondering if they were going to be sent to bed without their supper.

This story was written for an anthology of fictional solutions to real crimes; the writers were each asked to pick an unsolved mystery from the past and invent a solution. I chose Jack the Ripper. My angle on this was something that struck me as significantly revealing about the Ripper's victims. They'd all started out as respectable wives and mothers (the youngest victim, though childless, was pregnant). And they'd all been either abandoned or kicked out by their husbands. Deprived of the only role they knew how to play, they all had to turn to prostitution in order to survive. Every one of them had the same life story. I did not think this was coincidence. My "solution" is totally imaginary; I have no idea who Jack the Ripper was. None of the usual suggested suspects seem valid candidates as far as I can see.

JACK BE QUICK

30 September 1888, St. Jude's Vicarage, Whitechapel.

He took two, this time, and within the same hour, Inspector Abberline told us. The first victim was found this morning less than an hour after midnight, in a small court off Berner Street. The second woman was killed in Mitre Square forty-five minutes later. He did his hideous deed and escaped undetected, as he always does. Inspector Abberline believes he was interrupted in Berner Street, because he did not . . . do to that woman what he'd done to his other victims. My husband threw the Inspector a warning look, not wanting me exposed to such distressing matters more than necessary. "But the second woman was severely mutilated," Inspector Abberline concluded, offering no details. "He finished in Mitre Square what he'd begun in Berner Street."

My husband and I knew nothing of the double murder, not having left the vicarage all day. When no one appeared for morning services, Edward was angry. Customarily we can count on a Sunday congregation of a dozen or so; we should have suspected something was amiss. "Do you know who the women were, Inspector?" I asked.

"One of them," he said. "His Mitre Square victim was named Catherine Eddowes. We have yet to establish the identity of the Berner Street victim."

Inspector Abberline looked exhausted; I poured him another cup of tea. He undoubtedly would have preferred something stronger, but Edward permitted no spirits in the house, not even sherry. I waited until the Inspector had taken a sip before I put my next question to him. "Did he cut out Catherine Eddowes's womb the way he did Annie Chapman's?"

Edward looked shocked that I should know about that, but the police investigator was beyond shock. "Yes, Mrs. Wickham, he did. But this time he did not take it away with him."

It was one of the many concerns that baffled and horrified me about the series of grisly murders haunting London. Annie Chapman's disemboweled body had been found in Hanbury Street three weeks earlier; all the entrails had been piled above her shoulder except the womb. Why had he stolen her womb? "And the intestines?"

"Heaped over the left shoulder, as before."

Edward cleared his throat. "This Eddowes woman . . . she was a prostitute?"

Inspector Abberline said she was. "And I have no doubt that the Berner Street victim will prove to have been on the game as well. That's the only common ground among his victims—they were all prostitutes."

"Evil combating evil," Edward said with a shake of his head. "When will it end?"

Inspector Abberline put down his cup. "The end, alas, is not yet in sight. We are still conducting door-to-door searches, and the populace is beginning to panic. We have our hands full dispersing the mobs."

"Mobs?" Edward asked. "Has there been trouble?"

"I regret to say there has. Everyone is so desperate to find someone to blame . . ." The Inspector allowed the unfinished sentence to linger a moment. "Earlier today a constable was chasing a petty thief through the streets, and someone who saw them called out, 'It's the Ripper!' Several men joined in the chase, and then others, as the word spread that it was the Ripper the constable was pursuing. That mob was thirsting for blood—nothing less than a lynching would have satisfied them. The thief and the constable ended up barricading themselves in a building together until help could arrive."

Edward shook his head sadly. "The world has gone mad."

"It's why I have come to you, Vicar," Inspector Abberline said. "You can help calm them down. You could speak to them, persuade them to compose themselves. Your presence in the streets will offer a measure of reassurance."

"Of course," Edward said quickly. "Shall we leave now? I'll get my coat."

The Inspector turned to me. "Mrs. Wickham, thank you for the tea. Now we must be going." I saw both men to the door.

The Inspector did not know he had interrupted a disagreement between my husband and me, one that was recurring with increasing frequency of late. But I had no wish to revive the dispute when Edward returned; the shadow of these two new murders lay like a shroud over all other concerns. I retired to my sewing closet, where I tried to calm my spirit through prayer. One could not think dispassionately of this unknown man wandering the streets of London's East End, a man who hated women so profoundly that he cut away those parts of the bodies that proclaimed his victims to be female. I tried to pray for *him,* lost soul that he is; God forgive me, I could not.

1 October 1888, St. Jude's Vicarage.

Early the next morning the fog lay so thick about the vicarage that the street gaslights were still on. They performed their usual efficient function of lighting the *tops* of the poles; looking down from our bedroom window, I could not see the street below.

Following our morning reading from the Scriptures, Edward called my attention to an additional passage. "Since you are aware of what the Ripper does to his victims, Beatrice, it will be to your benefit to hear this. Attend. 'Let the breast be torn open and the heart and vitals be taken from hence and thrown over the shoulder.' "

A moment of nausea overtook me. "The same way Annie Chapman and the others were killed."

"Exactly," Edward said with a hint of triumph in his voice. "Those are Solomon's words, ordering the execution of three murderers. I wonder if anyone has pointed this passage out to Inspector Abberline? It could be of assistance in ascertaining the rationale behind these murders, perhaps revealing something of the killer's mental disposition . . ." He continued in this speculative vein for a while longer.

I was folding linen as I listened. When he paused for breath, I asked Edward about his chambray shirt. "I've not seen it these two weeks."

"Eh? It will turn up. I'm certain you have put it away somewhere."

I was equally certain I had not. Then, with some trepidation, I reintroduced the subject of our disagreement the night before. "Edward, would you be willing to reconsider your position concerning charitable donations? If parishioners can't turn to their church for help—"

"Allow me to interrupt you, my dear," he said. "I am convinced that suffering *cannot* be reduced by indiscriminately passing out money but only through the realistic appraisal of each man's problems. So long as the lower classes depend upon charity to see them through hard times, they will never learn thrift and the most propitious manner of spending what money they have."

Edward's "realistic appraisal" of individual problems always ended the same way, with little lectures on how to economize. "But surely in cases of extreme hardship," I said, "a small donation would not be detrimental to their future well-being."

"Ah, but how are we to determine who are those in true need? They will tell any lie to get their hands on a few coins which they promptly spend on hard drink. And then they threaten us when those coins are not forthcoming! This is the legacy my predecessor at St. Jude's has left us, this expectancy that the church *owes* them charity!"

That was true; the vicarage had been stoned more than once when Edward had turned petitioners away. "But the children, Edward—surely we can help the children! They are not to blame for their parents' wastrel ways."

Edward sat down next to me and took my hand. "You have a soft heart and a generous nature, Beatrice, and I venerate those qualities in you. Your natural instinct for charity is one of your most admirable traits." He smiled sadly. "Nevertheless, how will these poor, desperate creatures ever learn to care for their own children if we do it for them? And there is this. Has it not occurred to you that God may be testing *us?* How simple it would be, to hand out a few coins and convince ourselves we have done our Christian duty! No, Beatrice, God is asking more of us than that. We must hold firm in our resolve."

I acquiesced, seeing no chance of prevailing against such unshakable certitude that God's will was dictating our course of action. Furthermore, Edward Wickham was my husband and I owed him obedience, even when my heart was troubled and filled with uncertainty. It was his decision to make, not mine.

"Do not expect me until tea time," Edward said as he rose and went to fetch his greatcoat. "Mr. Lusk has asked me to attend a meeting of the Whitechapel Vigilance Committee, and I then have my regular calls to make. Best you not go out today, my dear, at least until Inspector Abberline has these riots under control." Edward's duties were keeping him away from the vicarage more and more. He sometimes would return in the early hours of the morning, melancholy and exhausted from trying to help a man find night work or from locating shelter for a homeless widow and her children. At times he seemed not to remember where he'd been; I was concerned for his health and his spirit.

The fog was beginning to lift by the time he departed, but I still could not see very far—except in my mind's eye.

If one were to proceed down Commercial Street and then follow Aldgate to Leadenhall and Cornhill on to the point where six roads meet at a statue of the Duke of Wellington, one would find oneself in front of the imposing Royal Exchange, its rich interior murals and Turkish floor paving a proper setting for the transactions undertaken there. Across Threadneedle Street, the Bank of England, with its windowless lower storeys, and the rocklike Stock Exchange both raise their impressive façades. Then one could turn to the opposite direction and behold several other banking establishments clustered around Mansion House, the Lord Mayor's residence. It still dumbfounds me to realize that the wealth of the nation is concentrated there, in so small an area . . . all within walking distance of the worst slums in the nation.

Do wealthy bankers ever spare a thought for the *appalling* poverty of Whitechapel and Spitalfields? The people living within the boundaries of St. Jude's parish are crowded like animals into a labyrinth of courts and alleys, none of which intersect major streets. The crumbling, hazardous buildings fronting the courts house complete families in each room, sometimes numbering as many as a dozen people; in such circumstances, incest is common . . . and, some say, inevitable. The buildings reek from the liquid sewage accumulated in the basements, while the courts themselves stink of garbage that attracts vermin, dogs, and other scavengers. Often one standing pipe in the courtyard serves as the sole source of water for all the inhabitants of three or four buildings, an outdoor pipe that freezes with unremitting regularity during the winter. Once Edward and I were called out in the middle of the night to succor a woman suffering from scarlet fever; we found her in a foul-smelling single room with three children and four pigs. Her husband, a cabman, had committed suicide the month before; and it wasn't until we were leaving that we discovered one of the children had been lying there dead for thirteen days.

The common lodging houses are even worse—filthy and infested and reservoirs of disease. In such doss houses a bed can be rented for fourpence for the night, strangers often sharing a bed because neither has the full price alone. There is no such thing as privacy, since the beds are lined up in crowded rows in the manner of dormitories. Beds are rented indiscriminately to men and women alike; consequently many of the doss houses are in truth brothels, and even those that are not have no compunction about renting a bed to a prostitute when she brings a paying customer with her. Inspector Abberline once told us the police estimate there are twelve hundred prostitutes in Whitechapel alone, fertile hunting grounds for the man who pleasures himself with the butchering of ladies of the night.

Ever since the Ripper began stalking the East End, Edward has been campaigning for more police to patrol the back alleys and for better street lighting. The problem is that Whitechapel is so poor it cannot afford the rates to pay for these needed improvements. If there is to be help, it must come from outside. Therefore I have undertaken a campaign of my own. Every day I write to philanthropists, charitable establishments, government officials. I petition every personage of authority and good will with whose name I am conversant, pleading the cause of the *children* of Whitechapel, especially those ragged, dirty street arabs who sleep wherever they can, eat whatever they can scavenge or steal, and perform every unspeakable act demanded of them in exchange for a coin they can call their own.

12 October 1888, Golden Lane Mortuary, City of London.

Today I did something I have never done before: I willfully disobeyed my husband. Edward had forbidden me to attend the inquest of Catherine Eddowes, saying I should not expose myself to such unsavory disclosures as were bound to be made. Also, he said it was unseemly for the vicar's wife to venture abroad unaccompanied, a dictum that impresses me as more appropriately belonging to another time and place. I waited until Edward left the vicarage and then hurried on my way. My path took me past one of the larger slaughterhouses in the area; with my handkerchief covering my mouth and nose to keep out the stench, I had to cross the road to avoid the blood and urine flooding the pavement. Once I had left Whitechapel, however, the way was unencumbered.

Outside the Golden Lane Mortuary I was pleased to encounter Inspector Abberline; he was surprised to see me there and immediately offered himself as my protector. "Is the Reverend Mr. Wickham not with you?"

"He has business in Shoreditch," I answered truthfully, not adding that Edward found inquests distasteful and would not have attended in any event.

"This crowd could turn ugly, Mrs. Wickham," Inspector Abberline said. "Let me see if I can obtain us two chairs near the door."

That he did, with the result that I had to stretch in a most unladylike manner to see over other people's heads. "Inspector," I said, "have you learned the identity of the other woman who was killed the same night as Catherine Eddowes?"

"Yes, it was Elizabeth Stride—Long Liz, they called her. About forty-five years of age and homely as sin, if you'll pardon my speaking ill of the dead. They were all unattractive, all the Ripper's victims. One thing is certain, he didn't choose them for their beauty."

"Elizabeth Stride was a prostitute?"

"That she was, Mrs. Wickham, I'm sorry to say. She had nine children somewhere, and a husband, until he could tolerate her drunkenness no longer and turned her out. A woman with a nice big family like that and a husband who supported them—what reasons could she have had to turn to drink?"

I could think of nine or ten. "What about Catherine Eddowes? Did she have children too?"

Inspector Abberline rubbed the side of his nose. "Well, she had a daughter, that much we know. We haven't located her yet, though."

The inquest was ready to begin. The small room was crowded, with observers standing along the walls and even outside in the passageway. The presiding coroner called the first witness, the police constable who found Catherine Eddowes's body.

The remarkable point to emerge from the constable's testimony was that his patrol took him through Mitre Square, where he'd found the body, every fourteen or fifteen minutes. The Ripper had only fifteen minutes to inflict so much damage? How swift he was, how sure of what he was doing!

It came out during the inquest that the Eddowes woman had been strangled before her killer had cut her throat, thus explaining why she had not cried out. In response to my whispered question, Inspector Abberline said yes, the other victims had also been strangled first. When the physicians present at the post mortem testified, they were agreed that the killer had sound anatomical knowledge but they were not in accord as to the extent of his actual skill in removing the organs. Their reports of what had been done to the body were disturbing; I grew slightly faint during the description of how the flaps of the abdomen had been peeled back to expose the intestines.

Inspector Abberline's sworn statement was succinct and free of speculation; he testified as to the course of action pursued by the police following the discovery of the body. There were other witnesses, people who had encountered Catherine Eddowes on the night she was killed. At one time she had been seen speaking to a middle-aged man wearing a black coat of good quality which was now slightly shabby; it was the same description that had emerged during the investigation of one of the Ripper's earlier murders. But at the end of it all we were no nearer to knowing the Ripper's identity than ever; the verdict was "Willful murder by some person unknown."

I refused Inspector Abberline's offer to have one of his assistants escort me home. "That makes six women he's killed now, this Ripper," I said. "You need all of your men for your investigation."

The Inspector rubbed the side of his nose, a mannerism I was coming to recognize indicated uncertainty. "As a matter of fact, Mrs. Wickham, I am of the opinion that only four were killed by the same man. You are thinking of the woman murdered near St. Jude's Church? And the one on Osborn Street?" He shook his head. "Not the Ripper's work, I'm convinced of it."

"What makes you think so, Inspector?"

"Because while those two women did have their throats cut, they weren't cut in the same manner as the later victims'. There is viciousness in the way the Ripper slashes his victims' throats . . . he is left-handed, we know, and he slashes twice, once each way. The cuts are deep, brutal . . . he almost took Annie Chapman's head off. No, Polly

Nichols was his first victim, then Chapman. And now this double murder, Elizabeth Stride and Catherine Eddowes. Those four are all the work of the same man."

I shuddered. "Did the four women know one another?"

"Not that we can determine," Inspector Abberline replied. "Evidently they had nothing in common except the fact that they were all four prostitutes."

More questions occurred to me, but I had detained the Inspector long enough. I bade him farewell and started back to St. Jude's, a long walk from Golden Lane. The daylight was beginning to fail, but I had no money for a hansom cab. I pulled my shawl tight about my shoulders and hurried my step, not wishing to be caught out of doors after dark. It was my husband's opinion that since the Ripper killed only prostitutes, respectable married women had nothing to fear. It was my opinion that my husband put altogether too much faith in the Ripper's ability to tell the difference.

I was almost home when a most unhappy incident ensued. A distraught woman approached me on Middlesex Street, carrying what looked like a bundle of rags which she thrust into my arms. Inside the rags was a dead baby. I cried out and almost dropped the cold little body.

"All he needed were a bit o' milk," the mother said, tears running down her cheeks.

"Oh, I am so sorry!" I gasped helplessly. The poor woman looked half-starved herself.

"They said it was no use a-sending to the church," she sobbed, "for you didn't never give nothing though you spoke kind."

I was so ashamed I had to lower my head. Even then I didn't have tuppence in my pocket to give her. I slipped off my shawl and wrapped it around the tiny corpse. "Bury him in this."

She mumbled something as she took the bundle from me and staggered away. She would prepare to bury her child in the shawl, but at the last moment she would snatch back the shawl's warmth for herself. She would cry over her dead baby as she did it, but she would do it. I prayed that she would do it.

16 October 1888, St. Jude's Vicarage.

This morning I paid an out-of-work bricklayer fourpence to clean out our fireplaces. In the big fireplace in the kitchen, he made a surprising discovery: soot-blackened buttons from my husband's missing chambray shirt turned up. When later I asked Edward why he had burned his best shirt, he looked at me in utter astonishment and demanded to know why I had burned it. Yet we two are the only ones living at the vicarage.

22 October 1888, Spitalfields Market.

The chemist regretfully informed me that the price of arsenic had risen, so of necessity I purchased less than the usual quantity, hoping Edward would find the diminished volume sufficient. Keeping the vicarage free of rats was costly. When first we took up residence at St. Jude's, we believed the rats were coming from the warehouses further along Commercial Street; but then we came to understand that every structure in Whitechapel was plagued with vermin. As fast as one killed them, others appeared to take their place.

A newspaper posted outside an alehouse caught my eye; I had made it a point to read every word published about the Ripper. The only new thing was that all efforts to locate the family of Catherine Eddowes, the Ripper's last victim, had failed. A front-page editorial demanded the resignation of the Commissioner of Police and various other men in authority. Three weeks had passed since the Ripper had taken two victims on the same night, and the police still had no helpful clues and no idea of who the Ripper was or when he would strike next. That he would strike again, no one doubted; that the police could protect the women of Whitechapel, no one believed.

In the next street I came upon a posted bill requesting anyone with information concerning the identity of the murderer to step forward and convey that information to the police. The request saddened me; the police could not have formulated a clearer admission of failure.

25 October 1888, St. Jude's Vicarage.

Edward is ill. When he had not appeared at the vicarage by tea time yesterday, I began to worry. I spent an anxious evening awaiting his return; it was well after midnight before I heard his key in the lock.

He looked like a stranger. His eyes were glistening and his clothes in disarray; his usual proud bearing had degenerated into a stoop, his shoulders hunched as if he were cold. The moment he caught sight of me he began berating me for failing to purchase the arsenic he needed to kill the rats; it was only when I led him to the pantry where he himself had spread the noxious powder around the rat holes did his reprimands cease. His skin was hot and dry, and with difficulty I persuaded him into bed.

But sleep would not come. I sat by the bed and watched him thrashing among the covers, throwing off the cool cloth

I had placed on his forehead. Edward kept waving his hands as if trying to fend someone off; what nightmares was he seeing behind those closed lids? In his delirium he began to cry out. At first the words were not clear, but then I understood my husband to be saying, "Whores! Whores! All whores!"

When by two in the morning his fever had not broken, I knew I had to seek help. I wrapped my cloak about me and set forth, not permitting myself to dwell on what could be hiding in the shadows. I do not like admitting it, but I was terrified; nothing less than Edward's illness could have driven me into the streets of Whitechapel at night. But I reached my destination with nothing untoward happening; I roused Dr. Phelps from a sound sleep and rode back to the vicarage with him in his carriage.

When Dr. Phelps bent over the bed, Edward's eyes flew open; he seized the doctor's upper arm in a grip that made the man wince. "They must be stopped!" my husband whispered hoarsely. "They . . . must be stopped!"

"We will stop them," Dr. Phelps replied gently and eased Edward's hand away. Edward's eyes closed and his body resumed its thrashing.

The doctor's examination was brief. "The fever is making him hallucinate," he told me. "Sleep is the best cure, followed by a period of bed rest." He took a small vial from his bag and asked me to bring a glass of water. He tapped a few drops of liquid into the water, which he then poured into Edward's mouth as I held his head.

"What did you give him?" I asked.

"Laudanum, to make him sleep. I will leave the vial with you." Dr. Phelps rubbed his right arm where Edward had gripped him. "Strange, I do not recall Mr. Wickham as being left-handed."

"He is ambidextrous. This fever . . . will he recover?"

"The next few hours will tell. Give him more laudanum only if he awakes in this same disturbed condition, and then only one drop in a glass of water. I will be back later to see how he is."

When Dr. Phelps had gone, I replaced the cool cloth on Edward's forehead and resumed my seat by the bed. Edward did seem calmer now, the wild thrashing at an end and only the occasional twitching of the hands betraying his inner turmoil. By dawn he was in a deep sleep and seemed less feverish.

My spirit was too disturbed to permit me to sleep. I decided to busy myself with household chores. Edward's black greatcoat was in need of a good brushing, so that came first. It was then that I discovered the rust-colored stains on the cuffs; they did not look fresh, but I could not be certain. Removing them was a delicate matter. The coat had seen better days and the cloth would not withstand vigorous handling. But eventually I got the worst of the stains out and hung the coat in the armoire.

Then I knelt by the bedroom window and prayed. I asked God to vanquish the dark suspicions that had begun to cloud my mind.

Whitechapel had changed Edward. Since he had accepted the appointment to St. Jude's, he had become more distant, more aloof. He had always been a reserved man, speaking rarely of himself and never of his past. I knew nothing of his childhood, only that he had been born in London; he had always discouraged my inquiring about the years before we met. If my parents had still been living when Edward first began to pay court, they would never have permitted me to entertain a man with no background, no family, and no connections. But by then I had passed what was generally agreed to be a marriageable age, and I was enchanted by the appearance out of nowhere of a gentleman of compatible spirit who desired me to spend my life with him. All I knew of Edward was that he was a little older than most new curates were, suggesting that he had started in some other profession, or had at least studied for one, before joining the clergy. Our twelve years together had been peaceful ones, and I had never regretted my choice.

But try as he might to disguise the fact, Edward's perspective had grown harsher during our tenure in Whitechapel. Sadly, he held no respect for the people whose needs he was here to minister to. I once heard him say to a fellow vicar, "The lower classes render no useful service. They create no wealth—more often they destroy it. They degrade whatever they touch, and as individuals are most probably incapable of improvement. Thrift and good management mean nothing to them. I resist terming them hopeless, but perhaps that is what they are." The Edward Wickham I married would never have spoken so.

"Beatrice."

I glanced toward the bed; Edward was awake and watching me. I rose from my knees and went to his side. "How do you feel, Edward?"

"Weak, as if I've lost a lot of blood." He looked confused. "Am I ill?"

I explained about the fever. "Dr. Phelps says you need a great deal of rest."

"Dr. Phelps? He was here?" Edward remembered nothing of the doctor's visit. Nor did he remember where he'd been the night before or even coming home. "This is frightening," he said shakily. His speech was slurred, an effect of the laudanum. "Hours of my life missing and no memory of them?"

"We will worry about that later. Right now you must try to sleep some more."

"Sleep . . . yes." I sat and held his hand until he drifted off again.

When he awoke a second time a few hours later, I brought him a bowl of broth, which he consumed with re-awakening appetite. My husband was clearly on the mend; he was considering getting out of bed when Dr. Phelps stopped by.

The doctor was pleased with Edward's progress. "Spend the rest of the day resting," he said, "and then tomorrow you may be allowed up. You must be careful not to overtax yourself or the fever may recur."

Edward put up a show of protesting, but I think he was secretly relieved that nothing was required of him except that he lie in bed all day. I escorted the doctor to the door.

"Make sure he eats," he said to me. "He needs to rebuild his strength."

I said I'd see to it. Then I hesitated; I could not go on without knowing. "Dr. Phelps, did anything happen last night?"

"I beg your pardon?"

He didn't know what I meant. "Did the Ripper strike again?"

Dr. Phelps smiled. "I am happy to say he did not. Perhaps we've seen an end of these dreadful killings, hmm?"

My relief was so great it was all I could do not to burst into tears. When the doctor had gone, I again fell to my knees and prayed, this time asking God to forgive me for entertaining such treacherous thoughts about my own husband.

1 November 1888, Leman Street Police Station, Whitechapel.

It was with a light heart that I left the vicarage this bright, crisp Tuesday morning. My husband was recovered from his recent indisposition and busy with his daily duties. I had received two encouraging replies to my petitions for charitable assistance for Whitechapel's children. And London had survived the entire month of October without another Ripper killing.

I was on my way to post two letters, my responses to the philanthropists who seemed inclined to listen to my plea. In my letters I had pointed out that over half the children born in Whitechapel die before they reach the age of five. The ones that do not die are mentally and physically underdeveloped; many of them that are taken into pauper schools are adjudged abnormally dull if not actual mental defectives. Children frequently arrive at school crying from hunger and then collapse at their benches. In winter they are too cold to think about learning their letters or doing their sums. The schools themselves are shamefully mismanaged and the children sometimes mistreated; there are school directors who pocket most of the budget and hire out the children to sweatshop owners as cheap labor.

What I proposed was the establishment of a boarding school for the children of Whitechapel, a place where the young would be provided with hygienic living conditions, wholesome food to eat, and warm clothing to wear—all before they ever set foot in a classroom. Then when their physical needs had been attended to, they would be given proper educational and moral instruction. The school was to be administered by an honest and conscientious director who could be depended upon never to exploit the downtrodden. All this would cost a great deal of money.

My letters went into the post accompanied by a silent prayer. I was then in Leman Street, not far from the police station. I stopped in and asked if Inspector Abberline was there.

He was; he greeted me warmly and offered me a chair. After inquiring after my husband's health, he sat back and looked at me expectantly.

Now that I was there, I felt a tinge of embarrassment. "It is presumptuous of me, I know," I said, "but may I make a suggestion? Concerning the Ripper, I mean. You've undoubtedly thought of every possible approach, but . . ." I didn't finish my sentence because he was laughing.

"Forgive me, Mrs. Wickham," he said, still smiling. "I would like to show you something." He went into another room and returned shortly carrying a large box filled with papers. "These are letters," he explained, "from concerned citizens like yourself. Each one offers a plan for capturing the Ripper. And we have two more boxes just like this one."

I flushed and rose to leave. "Then I'll not impose—"

"Please, Mrs. Wickham, take your seat. We read every letter that comes to us and give serious consideration to every suggestion made. I show you the box only to convince you we welcome suggestions."

I resumed my seat, not fully convinced but nevertheless encouraged by the Inspector's courtesy. "Very well." I tried to gather my thoughts. "The Ripper's first victim, you are convinced, was Polly Nichols?"

"Correct. Buck's Row, the last day of August."

"The *Illustrated Times* said that she was forty-two years old and separated from her husband, to whom she had borne five children. The cause of their separation was her propensity for strong drink. Mr. Nichols made his wife an allowance, according to the *Times*, until he learned of her prostitution—at which time he discontinued all pecuniary assistance. Is this account essentially correct?"

"Yes, it is."

"The Ripper's next victim was Annie Chapman, about forty, who was murdered early in September?"

"The night of the eighth," Inspector Abberline said, "although her body wasn't found until six the next morning. She was killed on Hanbury Street, less than half a mile from the Buck's Row site of Polly Nichols's murder."

I nodded. "Annie Chapman also ended on the streets because of drunkenness. She learned her husband had died only when her allowance stopped. When she tried to find her two children, she discovered they had been separated and sent to different schools, one of them abroad."

Inspector Abberline raised an eyebrow. "How did you ascertain that, Mrs. Wickham?"

"One of our parishioners knew her," I said. "Next came the double murder of Elizabeth Stride and Catherine Eddowes, during the small hours of the thirtieth of September. Berner Street and Mitre Square, a fifteen-minute walk from each other. The Stride woman was Swedish by birth and claimed to be a widow, but I have heard that may not be true. She was a notorious inebriate, according to one of the constables patrolling Fairclough Street, and she may simply have been ashamed to admit her husband would not allow her near the children—the *nine* children. Is this also correct?"

The Inspector was looking bemused. "It is."

"Of Catherine Eddowes I know very little. But the *Times* said she had spent the night before her death locked up in the Cloak Lane Police Station, because she'd been found lying drunk in the street somewhere in Aldgate. And you yourself told me she had a daughter. Did she also have a husband, Inspector?"

He nodded slowly. "A man named Conway. We've been unable to trace him."

The same pattern in each case. "You've said on more than one occasion that the four victims had only their prostitution in common. But in truth, Inspector, they had a great deal in common. They were all in their forties. They were all lacking in beauty. They had all been married. They all lost their homes through a weakness for the bottle." I took a breath. "And they were all mothers."

Inspector Abberline looked at me quizzically.

"They were all mothers *who abandoned their children*."

He considered it. "You think the Ripper had been abandoned?"

"Is it not possible? Or perhaps he too had a wife he turned out because of drunkenness. I don't know where he fits into the pattern. But consider. The nature of the murders makes it quite clear that these women are not just killed the way the unfortunate victim of a highwayman is killed—the women are being *punished*." I was uncomfortable speaking of such matters, but speak I must. "The manner of their deaths, one might say, is a grotesque version of the way they earned their livings."

The Inspector was also uncomfortable. "They were not raped, Mrs. Wickham."

"But of course they were, Inspector," I said softly. "They were raped with a knife."

I had embarrassed him. "We should not be speaking of this," he said, further chagrined at seeming to rebuke the vicar's wife. "These are not matters that concern you."

"All I ask is that you consider what I have said."

"Oh, I can promise you that," he answered wryly, and I

believed him. "I do have some encouraging news," he continued, desirous of changing the subject. "We have been given more men to patrol the streets—more than have ever before been concentrated in one section of London! The next time the Ripper strikes, we'll be ready for him."

"Then you think he will strike again."

"I fear so. He's not done yet."

It was the same opinion that was held by everyone else, but it was more ominous coming from the mouth of a police investigator. I thanked Inspector Abberline for his time and left.

The one thing that had long troubled me about the investigation of the Ripper murders was the refusal of the investigators to acknowledge that there was anything carnal about these violent acts. The killings were the work of a madman, the police and the newspapers agreed . . . as if that explained everything. But unless Inspector Abberline and the rest of those in authority could see the fierce hatred of women that drove the Ripper, I despaired of his ever being caught.

10 November 1888, Miller's Court, Spitalfields.

At three in the morning, I was still fully dressed, awaiting Edward's return to the vicarage. It had been hours since I'd made my last excuse to myself for his absence; his duties frequently kept him out late, but never this late. I was trying to decide whether I should go to Dr. Phelps for help when a frantic knocking started at the door.

It was a young market porter named Macklin who occasionally attended services at St. Jude's, and he was in a frantic state. "It's the missus," he gasped. " 'Er time is come and the midwife's too drunk to stand up. Will you come?"

I said I would. "Let me get a few things." I was distracted, wanting to send him away; but this was the Macklins' first child and I couldn't turn down his plea for help.

We hurried off in the direction of Spitalfields; the couple had recently rented a room in a slum building facing on Miller's Court. I knew the area slightly. Edward and I had once been called to a doss house there to minister to a dying man. That was the first time I'd ever been inside one of the common lodging houses; it was a big place, over three hundred beds and every one of them rented for the night.

Miller's Court was right across the street from the doss house. As we went into the courtyard, a girl of about twelve unfolded herself from the doorway where she had been huddled and tugged at my skirt. "Fourpence for a doss, lady?"

"Get out of 'ere!" Macklin yelled. "Go on!"

"Just a moment," I stopped him. I asked the girl if she had no home to go to.

"Mam turned me out," the girl answered sullenly. "Says don't come back 'til light."

I understood; frequently the women here put their children out on the street while they rented their room for immoral purposes. "I have no money," I told the girl, "but you may come inside."

"Not in my room, she don't!" Macklin shouted.

"She can be of help, Mr. Macklin," I said firmly.

He gave in ungraciously. The girl, who said her name was Rose Howe, followed us inside. Straightaway I started to sneeze; the air was filled with particles of fur. Someone in the building worked at plucking hair from dogs, rabbits, and perhaps even rats for sale to a furrier. There were other odors as well; the building held at least one fish that had not been caught yesterday. I could smell paste, from drying match boxes, most likely. It was all rather overpowering.

Macklin led us up a flight of stairs from which the banisters had been removed—for firewood, no doubt. Vermin-infested wallpaper was hanging in strips above our heads. Macklin opened a door upon a small room where his wife lay in labor. Mrs. Macklin was still a girl herself, only a few years older than Rose Howe. She was lying on a straw mattress, undoubtedly infested with fleas, on a broken-down bedstead. A few boxes were stacked against one wall; the only other piece of furniture was a plank laid across two stacks of bricks. I sent Macklin down to fill a bucket from the water pipe in the courtyard, and then I put Rose Howe to washing some rags I found in a corner.

It was a long labor. Rose curled up on the floor and went to sleep. Macklin wandered out for a few pints.

Day had broken before the baby came. Macklin was back, sobriety returning with each cry of pain from his young wife. Since it was daylight, Rose Howe could have returned to her own room but instead stayed and helped; she stood like a rock, letting Mrs. Macklin grip her thin wrists during the final bearing-down. The baby was undersized; but as I cleared out her mouth and nose, she voiced a howl that announced her arrival to the world in no uncertain terms. I watched a smile light the faces of both girls as Rose cleaned the baby and placed her in her mother's arms. Then Rose held the cord as I tied it off with thread in two places and cut it through with my sewing scissors.

Macklin was a true loving husband. "Don't you worry none, love," he said to his wife. "Next 'un'll be a boy."

I told Rose Howe I'd finish cleaning up and for her to go home. Then I told Macklin to bring his daughter to St. Jude's for christening. When at last I was ready to leave, the morning sun was high in the sky.

To my surprise the small courtyard was crowded with people, one of whom was a police constable. I tried to work my way through to the street, but no one would yield a passage for me; I'm not certain they even knew I was there. They were all trying to peer through the broken window of a ground-floor room. "Constable?" I called out. "What has happened here?"

He knew me; he blocked the window with his body and said, "You don't want to look in there, Mrs. Wickham."

A fist of ice closed around my heart; the constable's facial expression already told me, but I had to ask nonetheless. I swallowed and said, "Is it the Ripper?"

He nodded slowly. "It appears so, ma'am. I've sent for Inspector Abberline—you there, stand back!" Then, to me again: "He's not never killed indoors afore. This is new for him."

I was having trouble catching my breath. "That means . . . he didn't have to be quick this time. That means he could take as much time as he liked."

The constable was clenching and unclenching his jaw. "Yes'm. He took his time."

Oh dear God. "Who is she, do you know?"

"The rent-collector found her. Here, Thomas, what's her name again?"

A small, frightened-looking man spoke up. "Mary . . . Mary Kelly. Three months behind in 'er rent, she was. I thought she was hidin' from me."

The constable scowled. "So you broke the window to try to get in?"

" 'Ere, now, that winder's been broke these past six weeks! I pulled out the bit o' rag she'd stuffed in the hole so I could reach through and push back the curtain—just like you done, guv'ner, when you wanted to see in!" The rent-collector had more to say, but his words were drowned out by the growing noise of the crowd, which by now had so multiplied in its numbers that it overflowed from Miller's Court into a passageway leading to the street. A few women were sobbing, one of them close to screaming.

Inspector Abberline arrived with two other men, all three of them looking grim. The Inspector immediately tried the door and found it locked. "Break out the rest of the window," he ordered. "The rest of you, stand back. Mrs. Wickham, what are you doing here? Break in the window, I say!"

One of his men broke out the rest of the glass and crawled over the sill. We heard a brief, muffled cry, and then the door was opened from the inside. Inspector Abberline and his other man pushed into the room . . . and the latter abruptly rushed back out again, retching. The constable hastened to his aid, and without stopping to think about it, I stepped into the room.

What was left of Mary Kelly was lying on a cot next to a small table. Her throat had been cut so savagely that her head was nearly severed. Her left shoulder had been chopped through so that her arm remained attached to the body only by a flap of skin. Her face had been slashed and disfigured, and her nose had been hacked away . . . and carefully laid on the small table beside the cot. Her breasts had been sliced off and placed on the same table. The skin had been peeled from her forehead; her thighs had also been stripped of their skin. The legs themselves had been spread in an indecent posture and then slashed to the bone. And Mary Kelly's abdomen had been ripped open, and between her feet lay one of her internal organs . . . possibly the liver. On the table lay a piece of the victim's brown plaid woolen petticoat half-wrapped around still another organ. The missing skin had been carefully mounded on the table next to the other body parts, as if the Ripper were re-building his victim. But this time the killer had not piled the intestines above his victim's shoulder as he'd done before; this time, he had taken them away with him. Then as a final embellishment, he had pushed Mary Kelly's right hand into her ripped-open stomach.

Have you punished her enough, Jack? Don't you want to hurt her some more?

I felt a hand grip my arm and steer me firmly outside. "You shouldn't be in here, Mrs. Wickham," Inspector Abberline said. He left me leaning against the wall of the building as he went back inside; a hand touched my shoulder and Thomas the rent-collector said, "There's a place to sit, over 'ere." He led me to an upended wooden crate, where I sank down gratefully. I sat with my head bent over my knees for some time before I could collect myself enough to utter a prayer for Mary Kelly's soul.

Inspector Abberline's men were asking questions of everyone in the crowd. When one of them approached me, I explained I'd never known Mary Kelly and was here only because of the birth of the Macklin baby in the same building. The Inspector himself came over and commanded me to go home; I was not inclined to dispute the order.

"It appears this latest victim does not fit your pattern," the Inspector said as I was leaving. "Mary Kelly was a pros-titute, but she was still in her early twenties. And from what we've learned so far, she had no husband and no children."

So the last victim had been neither middle-aged, nor married, nor a mother. It was impossible to tell whether poor Mary Kelly had been homely or not. But the Ripper had clearly chosen a woman this time who was markedly different from his earlier victims, deviating from his customary pattern. I wondered what it meant; had some change taken place in his warped, evil mind? Had he progressed one step deeper into madness?

I thought about that on the way home from Miller's Court. I thought about that, and about Edward.

10 November 1888, St. Jude's Vicarage.

It was almost noon by the time I reached the vicarage. Edward was there, fast asleep. Normally he never slept during the day, but the small vial of laudanum Dr. Phelps had left was on the bedside table; Edward had drugged himself into a state of oblivion.

I picked up his clothes from the floor where he'd dropped them and went over every piece carefully; not a drop of blood anywhere. But the butchering of Mary Kelly had taken place indoors; the butcher could simply have removed his clothing before beginning his "work". Next I checked all the fireplaces, but none of them had been used to burn anything. It *could* be happenstance, I told myself. I didn't know how long Edward had been blacking out; it was probably not as singular as it seemed that one of his spells should coincide with a Ripper slaying. That's what I told myself.

The night had exhausted me. I had no appetite but a cup of fresh tea would be welcome. I was on my way to the kitchen when a knock at the door stopped me. It was the constable I'd spoken to at Miller's Court.

He handed me an envelope. "Inspector Abberline said to give you this." He touched his cap and was gone.

I went to stand by the window where the light was better.

Inside the envelope was a hastily scrawled note.

My dear Mrs. Wickham,

    Further information has come to light that makes it appear that your theory of a pattern in the Ripper murders may not be erroneous after all. Although Mary Kelly currently had no husband, she had at one time been married. At the age of sixteen she wed a collier who died less than a year later. During her widowhood she found a series of men to support her for brief periods until she ended on the streets. And she was given to strong drink, as the other four victims were. But the most cogent revelation is the fact that Mary Kelly was pregnant. That would explain why she was so much younger than the Ripper's earlier victims: he was stopping her before she could abandon her children.

                           Yrs,

                    Frederick Abberline

So. Last night the Ripper had taken two lives instead of one, assuring that a fertile young woman would never bear children to suffer the risk of being forsaken. It was not in the Ripper's nature to consider that his victims had themselves been abandoned in their time of need. Polly Nichols, Annie Chapman, Elizabeth Stride, and Catherine Eddowes had all taken to drink for reasons no one would ever know and had subsequently been turned out of their homes. And now there was Mary Kelly, widowed while little more than a child and with no livelihood—undoubtedly she lacked the education and resources to support herself honorably. Polly, Annie, Elizabeth, Catherine, and Mary . . . they had all led immoral and degraded lives, every one of them. But in not even one instance had it been a matter of choice.

    I put Inspector Abberline's note in a drawer in the

writing table and returned to the kitchen; I'd need to start a fire to make the tea. The wood box had recently been filled, necessitating my moving the larger pieces to get at the twigs underneath. Something else was underneath as well. I pulled out a long strip of brown plaid wool cloth with brown stains on it. Brown plaid wool. Mary Kelly's petticoat. Mary Kelly's blood.

The room began to whirl. There it was. No more making of excuses. No more denying the truth. I was married to the Ripper.

For twelve years Edward had kept the odious secret of his abnormal inner being, hiding behind a mask of gentility and even godliness. He had kept his secret well. But no more. The masquerade was ended. I sank to my knees and prayed for guidance. More than anything in the world I wanted to send for Inspector Abberline and have him take away the monster who was sleeping upstairs. But if the laudanum-induced sleep had the same effect this time as when he was ill, Edward would awake as his familiar rational self. If I could speak to him, make him understand what he'd done, give him the opportunity to surrender voluntarily to the police, surely that would be the most charitable act I could perform under these hideous circumstances. If Edward were to have any chance at all for redemption, he must beg both God and man for forgiveness.

With shaking hands I tucked the strip of cloth away in my pocket and forced myself to concentrate on the routine of making tea. The big kettle was already out; but when I went to fill it with water, it felt heavy. I lifted the lid and found myself looking at a pile of human intestines.

I did not faint . . . most probably because I was past all feeling by then. I tried to think. The piece of cloth Edward could have used to wipe off the knife; then he would have put the cloth in the wood box with the intention of burning it later. But why wait? And the viscera in the tea kettle . . . was I meant to find that? Was this Edward's way of asking for help? And where was the knife? Systematically I began to look for it; but after nearly two hours' intensive search, I found nothing. He could have disposed of the knife on his way home. He could have hidden it in the church. He could have it under his pillow.

I went into the front parlor and forced myself to sit down. I was frightened; I didn't want to stay under the same roof with him, I didn't want to fight for his soul. Did he even have a soul any more? The Edward Wickham I had lain beside every night for twelve years was a counterfeit person, one whose carefully fabricated personality and demeanor had been devised to control and constrain the demon imprisoned inside. The deception had worked well until we came to Whitechapel, when the constraints began to weaken and the demon escaped. What had caused the change—was it the place itself? The constant presence of prostitutes in the streets? It was beyond my comprehension.

The stresses of the past twenty-four hours eventually proved too much for me; my head fell forward, and I slept.

Edward's hand on my shoulder awoke me. I started, and gazed at him with apprehension; but his face showed only gentle concern. "Is something wrong, Beatrice? Why are you sleeping in the afternoon?"

I pressed my fingertips against my eyes. "I did not sleep last night. The Macklin baby was born early this morning."

"Ah! Both mother and child doing well, I trust? I hope you impressed upon young Macklin the importance of an early christening. But Beatrice, the next time you are called out, I would be most grateful if you could find a way to send me word. When you had not returned by midnight, I began to grow worried."

That was the first falsehood Edward had ever told me that I could recognize as such; it was I who had been waiting for him at midnight. His face was so open, so seemingly free of guile . . . did he honestly have no memory of the night before, or was he simply exceptionally skilled in the art of deception? I stood up and began to pace. "Edward, we must talk about last night . . . about what you did last night."

His eyebrow shot up. "I?"

I couldn't look at him. "I found her intestines in the tea kettle. Mary Kelly's intestines."

"Intestines?" I could hear the distaste in his voice. "What is this, Beatrice? And who is Mary Kelly?"

"She's the woman you killed last night!" I cried. "Surely you knew her name!" I turned to confront him . . . and saw a look of such loathing on his face that I took a step back. "Oh!" I gasped involuntarily. "Please don't . . ." Edward? Jack?

The look disappeared immediately—he knew, he knew what he was doing! "I killed someone last night, you say?" he asked, his rational manner quickly restored. "And then I put her intestines . . . in the teakettle? Why don't you show me, Beatrice?"

Distrustful of his suggestion, I nevertheless led the way to the kitchen. As I'd half expected, the teakettle was empty and spotlessly clean. With a heavy heart I pulled the piece of brown plaid cloth out of my pocket. "But here is something you neglected to destroy."

He scowled. "A dirty rag?"

"Oh, Edward, stop professing you know nothing of this! It is a strip from Mary Kelly's petticoat, as you well realize!

Edward, you must go to the police. Confess all, make your peace with God. No one else can stop your nocturnal expeditions—you must stop yourself! Go to Inspector Abberline."

He held out one hand. "Give me the rag," he said expressionlessly.

"Think of your soul, Edward! This is your one chance for salvation! You *must* confess!"

"The rag, Beatrice."

"I cannot! Edward, do you not understand? You are accursed—your own actions have damned you! You must go down on your knees and beg for forgiveness!"

Edward lowered his hand. "You are ill, my dear. This delusion of yours that I am the Ripper—that is the crux of your accusation, is it not? This distraction is most unbefitting the wife of the vicar of St. Jude's. I cannot tolerate the thought that before long you may be found raving in the street. We will pray together, we will ask God to send you self-control."

I thought I understood what that meant. "Very well . . . if you will not turn yourself over to the police, there is only one alternate course of action open to you. You must kill yourself."

"Beatrice!" He was shocked. "Suicide is a *sin!*"

His reaction was so absurd that I had to choke down a hysterical laugh. But it made me understand that further pleading would be fruitless. He was hopelessly insane; I would never be able to reach him.

Edward was shaking his head. "I am most disturbed, Beatrice. This dementia of yours is more profound than I realized. I must tell you I am unsure of my capacity to care for you while you are subject to delusions. Perhaps an institution is the rightful solution."

I was stunned. "You would put me in an asylum?"

He sighed. "Where else will we find physicians qualified to treat dementia? But if you cannot control these delusions of yours, I see no other recourse. You must pray, Beatrice, you must pray for the ability to discipline your thoughts."

He *could* have me locked away; he could have me locked away and then continue unimpeded with his ghastly killings, never having to worry about a wife who noticed too much. It was a moment before I could speak. "I will do as you say, Edward. I will pray."

"Excellent! I will pray with you. But first—the rag, please."

Slowly, reluctantly, I handed him the strip of Mary Kelly's petticoat. Edward took a fireplace match and struck it, and the evidence linking him to murder dissolved into thin black smoke that spiraled up the chimney. Then we prayed; we asked God to give me the mental and spiritual willpower I lacked.

Following that act of hypocrisy, Edward suggested that I prepare our tea; I put the big teakettle aside and used my smaller one. Talk during tea was about several church duties Edward still needed to perform. I spoke only when spoken to and was careful to give no offense. I did everything I could to assure my husband that I deferred to his authority.

Shortly before six Edward announced he was expected at a meeting of the Whitechapel Vigilance Committee. I waited until he was out of sight and went first to the cupboard for a table knife and then to the writing table for a sheet of foolscap. Then I stepped into the pantry and began to scrape up as much of the arsenic from the rat holes as I could.

23 February 1892, Whitechapel Charitable Institute for Indigent Children.

Inspector Abberline sat in my office, nodding approval at everything he'd seen. "It's difficult to believe," he said, "that these are the same thin and dirty children who only months ago used to sleep in doorways and under wooden crates. You have worked wonders, Mrs. Wickham. The board of trustees could not have found a better director. Are the children learning to read and write? *Can* they learn?"

"Some can," I answered. "Others are slower. The youngest are the quickest, it seems. I have great hopes for them."

"I wonder if they understand how fortunate they are. What a pity the Reverend Mr. Wickham didn't live to see this. He would have been so pleased with what you've accomplished."

"Yes." Would he have? Edward always believed the poor should care for their own.

The Inspector was still thinking of my late husband. "I had an aunt who succumbed to gastric fever," he said. "Dreadful way to die, dreadful." He suddenly realized I might not care to be reminded of the painful method of Edward's passing. "I do beg your pardon—that was thoughtless of me."

I told him not to be concerned. "I am reconciled to his death now, as much as I can ever be. My life is here now, in the school, and it is a most rewarding way to spend my days."

He smiled. "I can see you are in your element." Then he sobered. "I came not only to see your school but also to tell you something." He leaned forward in his chair. "The file on the Ripper is officially closed. It's been more than two years since his last murder. For whatever reason he stopped, he *did* stop. That particular reign of terror is over. The case is closed."

My heart lifted. Keeping up my end of the conversation, I asked, "Why do you think he stopped, Inspector?"

He rubbed the side of his nose. "He stopped either because he's dead or because he's locked up somewhere, in an asylum or perhaps in prison for some other crime. Forgive my bluntness, Mrs. Wickham, but I earnestly hope it is the former. Inmates have been known to escape from asylums and prisons."

"I understand. Do you think the file will ever be reopened?"

"Not for one hundred years. Once a murder case is marked closed, the files are sealed and the date is written on the outside when they can be made public. It will be a full century before anyone looks at those papers again."

It couldn't be more official than that; the case was indeed closed. "A century . . . why so long a time?"

"Well, the hundred-year rule was put into effect to guarantee the anonymity of all those making confidential statements to the police during the course of the investigation. It's best that way. Now no one will be prying into our reports on the Ripper until the year 1992. It is over."

"Thank Heaven for that."

"Amen."

Inspector Abberline chatted a little longer and then took his leave. I strolled through the halls of my school, a former church building adapted to its present needs. I stopped in one of the classrooms. Some of the children were paying attention to the teacher, others were daydreaming, a few were drawing pictures. Just like children everywhere.

Not all the children who pass through here will be helped; some will go on to better themselves, but others will slide back into the life of the streets. I can save none of them. I must not add arrogance to my other offenses by assuming the role of deliverer; God does not entrust the work of salvation to one such as I. But I am permitted to offer the children a chance, to give them the opportunity to lift themselves above the life of squalor and crime that is all they have ever known. I do most earnestly thank God for granting me this privilege.

Periodically I return to Miller's Court. I go there not because it is the site of Edward's final murder, but because it is where I last saw Rose Howe, the young girl who helped me deliver the Macklin baby. There is a place for Rose in my school. I have not found her yet, but I will keep searching.

My life belongs to the children of Whitechapel now. My prayers are for them; those prayers are the only ones of mine ever likely to be answered. When I do pray for myself, it is always and only to ask for an easier place in Hell.